Three Women

Ella Wheeler Wilcox

Contents

THREE WOMEN

BY

Ella Wheeler Wilcox

THREE WOMEN

My love is young, so young;
  Young is her cheek, and her throat,
And life is a song to be sung
  With love the word for each note.

Young is her cheek and her throat;
  Her eyes have the smile o' May.
And love is the word for each note
  In the song of my life to-day.

Her eyes have the smile o' May;
  Her heart is the heart of a dove,
And the song of my life to-day
  Is love, beautiful love.

Her heart is the heart of a dove,
  Ah, would it but fly to my breast
Where lone, beautiful love,
  Has made it a downy nest.

Ah, would she but fly to my breast,
  My love who is young, so young;
I have made her a downy nest
  And life is a song to be sung.

THREE WOMEN.

I.

A dull little station, a man with the eye
Of a dreamer; a bevy of girls moving by;
A swift moving train and a hot Summer sun,
The curtain goes up, and our play is begun.
The drama of passion, of sorrow, of strife,
Which always is billed for the theatre Life.
It runs on forever, from year unto year,
With scarcely a change when new actors appear.
It is old as the world is--far older in truth,
For the world is a crude little planet of youth.
And back in the eras before it was formed,
The passions of hearts through the Universe stormed.

Maurice Somerville passed the cluster of girls
Who twisted their ribbons and fluttered their curls
In vain to attract him; his mind it was plain
Was wholly intent on the incoming train.
That great one eyed monster puffed out its black breath,
Shrieked, snorted and hissed, like a thing bent on death,
Paused scarcely a moment, and then sped away,
And two actors more now enliven our play.

A graceful young woman with eyes like the morn,
With hair like the tassels which hang from the corn,
And a face that might serve as a model for Peace,
Moved lightly along, smiled and bowed to Maurice,
Then was lost in the circle of friends waiting near.
A discord of shrill nasal tones smote the ear,
As they greeted their comrade and bore her from sight.
(The ear oft is pained while the eye feels delight
In the presence of women throughout our fair land:
God gave them the graces which win and command,
But the devil, who always in mischief rejoices,
Slipped into their teachers and ruined their voices.)

There had stepped from the train just behind Mabel Lee
A man whose deportment bespoke him to be
A child of good fortune. His mien and his air
Were those of one all unaccustomed to care.
His brow was not vexed with the gold seeker's worry,
His manner was free from the national hurry.
Repose marked his movements. Yet gaze in his eye,
And you saw that this calm outer man was a lie;
And you knew that deep down in the depths of his breast
There dwelt the unmerciful imp of unrest.

He held out his hand; it was clasped with a will
In both the firm palms of Maurice Somerville.
"Well, Reese, my old Comrade;" "Ha, Roger, my boy,"
They cried in a breath, and their eyes gemmed with joy
(Which but for their sex had been set in a tear),
As they walked arm in arm to the trap waiting near,
And drove down the shining shell roadway which wound
Through forest and meadow, in search of the Sound.

Roger:

I smell the salt water--that perfume which starts
The blood from hot brains back to world withered hearts;
You may talk of the fragrance of flower filled fields,
You may sing of the odors the Orient yields,
You may tell of the health laden scent of the pine,
But give me the subtle salt breath of the brine.
Already I feel lost emotions of youth
Steal back to my soul in their sweetness and truth;
Small wonder the years leave no marks on your face,
Time's scythe gathers rust in this idyllic place.
You must feel like a child on the Great Mother's breast,
With the Sound like a nurse watching over your rest?

Maurice:

There is beauty and truth in your quaint simile,
I love the Sound more than the broad open sea.
The ocean seems always stern, masculine, bold,
The Sound is a woman, now warm, and now cold.
It rises in fury and threatens to smite,
Then falls at your feet with a coo of delight;
Capricious, seductive, first frowning, then smiling,
And always, whatever its mood is, beguiling.
Look, now you can see it, bright beautiful blue,
And far in the distance there loom into view
The banks of Long Island, full thirty miles off;
A sign of wet weather to-morrow. Don't scoff!
We people who chum with the waves and the wind
Know more than all wise signal bureaus combined.

But come, let us talk of yourself--for of me
There is little to tell which your eyes may not see.
Since we finished at College (eight years, is it not?)
I simply have dreamed away life in this spot.
With my dogs and my horses, a book and a pen,
And a week spent in town as a change now and then.
Fatigue for the body, disease for the mind,
Are all that the city can give me, I find.
Yet once in a while there is wisdom I hold
In leaving the things that are dearer than gold,--
Loved people and places--if only to learn
The exquisite rapture it is to return.
But you, I remember, craved motion and change;
You hated the usual, worshiped the strange.
Adventure and travel I know were your theme:
Well, how did the real compare with the dream?
You have compassed the earth since we parted at Yale,
Has life grown the richer, or only grown stale?

Roger:

Stale, stale, my dear boy! that's the story in short,
I am weary of travel, adventure and sport;
At home and abroad, in all climates and lands,
I have had what life gives when a full purse commands,
I have chased after Pleasure, that phantom faced elf,
And lost the best part of my youth and myself.
And now, barely thirty, I'm heart sick and blue;
Life seems like a farce scarcely worth sitting through.
I dread its long stretch of dissatisfied years;
Ah! wealth is not always the boon it appears.
And poverty lights not such ruinous fires
As gratified appetites, tastes and desires.

Fate curses, when letting us do as we please--
It stunts a man's soul to be cradled in ease.

Maurice:

You are right in a measure; the devil I hold
Is oftener found in full coffers of gold
Than in bare, empty larders. The soul, it is plain,
Needs the conflicts of earth, needs the stress and the strain
Of misfortune, to bring out its strength in this life--
The Soul's calisthenics are sorrow and strife.
But, Roger, what folly to stand in youth's prime
And talk like a man who could father old Time.
You have life all before you; the past,--let it sleep;
Its lessons alone are the things you should keep.
There is virtue sometimes in our follies and sinnings;
Right lives very often have faulty beginnings.
Results, and not causes, are what we should measure.
You have learned precious truths in your search after pleasure.

You have learned that a glow worm is never a star,
You have learned that Peace builds not her temples afar.
And now, dispossessed of the spirit to roam,
You are finely equipped to establish a home.
That's the one thing you need to lend savor to life,
A home, and the love of a sweet hearted wife,
And children to gladden the path to old age.

Roger:

Alas! from life's book I have torn out that page;
I have loved many times and in many a fashion,
Which means I know nothing at all of the passion.

I have scattered my heart, here and there, bit by bit,
'Til now there is nothing worth while left of it;
And, worse than all else, I have ceased to believe
In the virtue and truth of the daughters of Eve.
There's tragedy for you--when man's early trust
In woman, experience hurls to the dust!

Maurice:

Then you doubt your own mother?

Roger:

      She passed heavenward
Before I remember; a saint, I have heard,
While she lived; there are scores of good women to-day,
Temptation has chanced not to wander their way.
The devil has more than his lordship can do,
He can't make the rounds, so some women keep true.

Maurice:

You think then each woman, if tempted, must fall?

Roger:

Yes, if tempted her way--not one way suits them all--
They have tastes in their sins as they have in their clothes,
The tempter, of course, has to first study those.
One needs to be flattered, another is bought;
One yields to caresses, by frowns one is caught.
One wants a bold master, another a slave,
With one you must jest, with another be grave.

But swear you're a sinner whom she has reformed
And the average feminine fortress is stormed.
In rescuing men from abysses of sin
She loses her head--and herself tumbles in.
The mind of a woman was shaped for a saint,
But deep in her heart lies the devil's own taint.
With plans for salvation her busy brain teems,
While her heart longs in secret to know how sin seems.
And if with this question unanswered she dies,
Temptation came not in the right sort of guise.
There's my estimate, Reese, of the beautiful sex;
I see by your face that my words wound and vex,
But remember, my boy, I'm a man of the world.

Maurice:

Thank God, in the vortex I have not been hurled.
If experience breeds such a mental disease,
I am glad I have lived with the birds and the bees,
And the winds and the waves, and let people alone
So far in my life but good women I've known.
My mother, my sister, a few valued friends--
A teacher, a schoolmate, and there the list ends.
But to know one true woman in sunshine and gloom,
From the zenith of life to the door of the tomb,
To know her, as I knew that mother of mine,
Is to know the whole sex and to kneel at the shrine.

Roger:

Then you think saint and woman synonymous terms?

Maurice:

Oh, no! we are all, men and women, poor worms
Crawling up from the dampness and darkness of clay
To bask in the sunlight and warmth of the day.
Some climb to a leaf and reflect its bright sheen,
Some toil through the grass, and are crushed there unseen.
Some sting if you touch them, and some evolve wings;
Yet God dwells in each of the poor, groping things.
They came from the Source--to the Source they go back;
The sinners are those who have missed the true track.
We can not judge women or men as a class,
Each soul has its own distinct place in the mass.

There is no sex in sin; it were folly to swear
All women are angels, but worse to declare
All are devils as you do. You're morbid, my boy,
In what you thought gold you have found much alloy
And now you are doubting there is the true ore.
But wait till you study my sweet simple store
Of pure sterling treasures; just wait till you've been
A few restful weeks, or a season, within
The charmed circle of home life; then, Roger, you'll find
These malarial mists clearing out of your mind.
As a ship cuts the fog and is caught by the breeze,
And swept through the sunlight to fair, open seas,
So your heart will be caught and swept out to the ocean
Of youth and youth's birthright of happy emotion.
I'll wager my hat (it was new yesterday)
That you'll fall in love, too, in a serious way.
Our girls at Bay Bend are bewitching and fair,
And Cupid lurks ever in salt Summer air.

Roger:

I question your gifts as a prophet, and yet,
I confess in my travels I never have met
A woman whose face so impressed me at sight,
As one seen to-day; a mere girl, sweet and bright,
Who entered the train quite alone and sat down
Surrounded by parcels she'd purchased in town.
A trim country lass, but endowed with the beauty
Which makes a man think of his conscience and duty.
Some women, you know, move us that way--God bless them,
While others rouse only a thirst to possess them
The face of the girl made me wish to be good,
I went out and smoked to escape from the mood.
When conscience through half a man's life has been sleeping
What folly to wake it to worry and weeping!

Maurice:

The pessimist role is a modern day fad,
But, Roger, you make a poor cynic, my lad.
Your heart at the core is as sound as a nut,
Though the wheels of your mind have dropped into the rut
Of wrong thinking. You need a strong hand on the lever
Of good common sense, and an earnest endeavor
To pull yourself out of the slough of despond
Back into the highway of peace just beyond.
And now, here we are at Peace Castle in truth,
And there stands its Chatelaine, sweet Sister Ruth,
To welcome you, Roger; you'll find a new type
In this old-fashioned girl, who in years scarcely ripe,
And as childish in heart as she is in her looks,
And without worldly learning or knowledge of books,

Yet in housewifely wisdom is wise as a sage.
She is quite out of step with the girls of her age,
For she has no ambition beyond the home sphere.
Ruth, here's Roger Montrose, my comrade of dear
     College days.

The gray eyes of the girl of nineteen
Looked into the face oft in fancy she'd seen
When her brother had talked of his comrade at Yale.
His stature was lower, his cheek was more pale
Than her thought had portrayed him; a look in his eye
Made her sorry, she knew not for what nor knew why,
But she longed to befriend him, as one needing aid
While he, gazing down on the face of the maid,
Spoke some light words of greeting, the while his mind ran
On her "points" good and bad; for the average man
When he looks at a woman proceeds first to scan her
As if she were horse flesh, and in the same manner
Notes all that is pleasing, or otherwise. So
Roger gazed at Ruth Somerville.

               "Mouth like a bow
And eyes full of motherhood; color too warm,
And too round in the cheek and too full in the form
For the highest ideal of beauty and art.
Domestic--that word is the cue to her part
She would warm a man's slippers, but never his veins;
She would feed well his stomach, but never his brains.
And after she looks on her first baby's face,
Her husband will hold but a second-class place
In her thoughts or emotions, unless he falls ill,
When a dozen trained nurses her place can not fill.
She is sweet of her kind; and her kind since the birth

Of this sin ridden, Circe-cursed planet, the Earth,
Has kept it, I own, with its medleys of evil
From going straight into the hands of the devil.
It is not through its heroes the world lives and thrives,
But through its sweet commonplace mothers and wives.
We love them, and leave them; deceive, and respect them,
We laud loud their virtues and straightway neglect them.
They are daisy and buttercup women of earth
Who grace common ways with their sweetness and worth.
We praise, but we pass them, to reach for some flower
That stings when we pluck it, or wilts in an hour.

"You are thornless, fair Ruth! you are useful and sweet!
But lovers shall pass you to sigh at the feet
Of the selfish and idle, for such is man's way;
Your lot is to work, and to weep, and to pray.
To give much and get little; to toil and to wait
For the meager rewards of indifferent fate.
Yet so wholesome your heart, you will never complain;
You will feast on life's sorrow and drink of its pain,
And thank God for the banquet; 'tis women like you
Who make the romancing of preachers seem true.
The earth is your debtor to such large amounts
There must be a heaven to square up accounts,
Or else the whole scheme of existence at best
Is a demon's poor effort at making a jest."

That night as Ruth brushed out her bright hazel hair
Her thoughts were of Roger, "His bold laughing air
Is a cloak to some sorrow concealed in his breast,
His mind is the home of some secret unrest."

She sighed; and there woke in her bosom once more

The impulse to comfort and help him; to pour
Soothing oil from the urn of her heart on his wounds.
Where motherhood nature in woman abounds
It is thus Cupid comes; unannounced and unbidden,
In sweet pity's guise, with his arrows well hidden.
But once given welcome and housed as a guest,
He hurls the whole quiver full into her breast,
While he pulls off his mask and laughs up in her eyes
With an impish delight at her start of surprise.
So intent is this archer on bagging his game
He scruples at nothing which gives him good aim.

Ruth's heart was a virgin's, in love menaced danger
While she sat by her mirror and pitied the stranger.
But just as she blew out her candle and stood
Robed for sleep in the moonlight, a change in her mood
Quickly banished the dreamer, and brought in its stead
The practical housekeeper. Sentiment fled;
And she puzzled her brain to decide which were best,
Corn muffins or hot graham gems, for the guest!

II.

The short-sighted minister preached at Bay Bend
His long-winded sermon quite through to the end,
Unmindful there sat in the Somerville pew
A stranger whose pale handsome countenance drew
All eyes from his own reverend self; nor suspected
What Ruth and her brother too plainly detected
That the stranger was bored.

      "Though his gaze never stirred
From the face of the preacher, his heart has not heard,"
Ruth said to herself; and her soft mother-eye
Was fixed on his face with a look like a sigh
In its tremulous depths, as they rose to depart.
Then suddenly Roger, alert, seemed to start
And his dull, listless glance changed to one of surprise
And of pleasure. Ruth saw that the goal of his eyes
Was her friend Mabel Lee in the vestibule; fair
As a saint that is pictured with sun tangled hair
And orbs like the skies in October. She smiled,
And the saint disappeared in the innocent child
With an unconscious dower of beauty and youth
She paused in the vestibule waiting for Ruth
And seemed not to notice the warm eager gaze
Of two men fixed upon her in different ways.
One, the look which souls lift to a being above,
The other a look of unreasoning love
Born of fancy and destined to grow in an hour
To a full fledged emotion of mastering power.

She spoke, and her voice disappointed the ear;
It lacked some deep chords that the heart hoped to hear.
It was sweet, but not vibrant; it came from the throat,
And one listened in vain for a full chested note.
While something at times like a petulant sound
Seemed in strange disaccord with the peace so profound
Of the eyes and the brow.

      Though our sight is deceived
The ear is an organ that may be believed.
The faces of people are trained to conceal,
But their unruly voices are prone to reveal
What lies deep in their natures; a voice rarely lies,
But Mabel Lee's voice told one tale, while her eyes
Told another. Large, liquid, and peaceful as lakes
Where the azure dawn rests, ere the loud world awakes,
Were the beautiful eyes of the maiden. "A saint,
Without mortal blemish or weak human taint,"
Said Maurice to himself. To himself Roger said:
"The touch of her soft little hands on my head
Would convert me. What peace for a world weary breast
To just sit by her side and be soothed into rest."

Daring thoughts for a stranger. Maurice, who had known
Mabel Lee as a child, to himself would not own
Such bold longings as those were. He held her to be
Too sacred for even a thought that made free.
And the voice in his bosom was silenced and hushed
Lest the bloom from her soul by his words should be brushed.

There are men to whom love is religion; but woman
Is far better pleased with a homage more human.
Though she may not be able to love in like fashion,

She wants to be wooed with both ardor and passion.
Had Mabel Lee read Roger's thoughts of her, bold
Though they were, they had flattered and pleased her, I hold.

The stranger was duly presented.

Roger:

　　　　Miss Lee,
I am sure, has no least recollection of me,
But the pleasure is mine to have looked on her face
Once before this.

Mabel:

　　　　Indeed? May I ask where?

Roger:

　　　　The place
Was the train, and the time yesterday.

Mabel:

　　　　"Then I came
From my shopping excursion in town by the same
Fast express which brought you? Had I known that the friend
Of my friends, was so near me en route for Bay Bend,
I had waived all conventions and asked him to take
One-half of my parcels for sweet pity's sake.

Roger:

You sadden me sorely. As long as I live
I shall mourn the great pleasure chance chose not to give.

Maurice:

Take courage, mon ami. Our fair friend, Miss Lee,
Fills her time quite as full of sweet works as the bee;
Like the bee, too, she drives out the drones from her hive.
You must toil in her cause, in her favor to thrive.

Roger:

She need but command me. To wait upon beauty
And goodness combined makes a pleasure of duty.

Maurice:

Who serves Mabel Lee serves all Righteousness too.
Pray, then, that she gives you some labor to do.
The cure for the pessimist lies in good deeds.
Who toils for another forgets his own needs,
And mischief and misery never attend
On the man who is occupied fully.

Ruth:

       Our friend
Has the town on her shoulders. Whatever may be
The cause that is needy, we look to Miss Lee.
Have you gold? She will make you disgorge it ere long;
Are you poor? Well, perchance you can dance--sing a song--

Make a speech--tell a story, or plan a charade.
Whatever you have, gold or wits, sir, must aid
In her numerous charities.

Mabel:

   Riches and brain
Are but loans from the Master. He meant them, 'tis plain,
To be used in His service; and people are kind,
When once you can set them to thinking. I find
It is lack of perception, not lack of good heart
Which makes the world selfish in seeming. My part
Is to call the attention of Plenty to need,
And to bid Pleasure pause for a moment and heed
The woes and the burdens of Labor.

Roger:

   One plea
From the rosy and eloquent lips of Miss Lee
Would make Avarice pour out his coffers of gold
At her feet, I should fancy; would soften the cold,
Selfish heart of the world to compassionate sighs,
And bring tears of pity to vain Pleasure's eyes.

As the sunset a color on lily leaves throws,
The words and the glances of Roger Montrose
O'er the listener's cheeks sent a pink tinted wave;
While Maurice seemed disturbed, and his sister grew grave.
The false chink of flattery's coin smites the ear
With an unpleasant ring when the heart is sincere.
Yet the man whose mind pockets are filled with this ore,
Though empty his brain cells, is never a bore

To the opposite sex.

      While Maurice knew of old
Roger's wealth in that coin that does duty for gold
In Society dealings, it hurt him to see
The cheap metal offered to sweet Mabel Lee.

(Yet, perchance, the hurt came, not so much that 'twas offered,
As in seeing her take, with a smile, what was proffered.)
They had walked, two by two, down the elm shaded street,
Which led to a cottage, vine hidden, and sweet
With the breath of the roses that covered it, where
Mabel paused in the gateway; a picture most fair.
"I would ask you to enter," she said, "ere you pass,
But in just twenty minutes my Sunday-school class
Claims my time and attention; and later I meet
A Committee on Plans for the boys of the street.
We seek to devise for these pupils in crime
Right methods of thought and wise uses of time.

Roger:

I am but a vagrant, untutored and wild,
May I join your street class, and be taught like a child?

Mabel:

If you come I will carefully study your case.

Maurice:

I must go along, too, just to keep him in place.

Mabel:

Then you think him unruly?

Maurice:

Decidedly so.

Roger:

I was, but am changed since one-half hour ago.

Mabel:

The change is too sudden to be of much worth;
The deepest convictions are slowest of birth.
Conversion, I hold, to be earnest and lasting,
Begins with repentance and praying and fasting,
And (begging your pardon for such a bold speech),
You seem, sir, a stranger to all and to each
Of these ways of salvation.

Roger:

Since yesterday, miss,
When, unseen, I first saw you (believe me in this),
I have deeply repented my sins of the past.
To-night I will pray, and to-morrow will fast--
Or, make it next week, when my shore appetite
May be somewhat subdued in its ravenous might.

Maurice:

That's the way of the orthodox sinner! He waits
Until time or indulgence or misery sates
All his appetites, then his repentance begins,
When his sins cease to please, then he gives up his sins
And grows pious. Now prove you are morally brave
By actually giving up something you crave!
We have fricasseed chicken and strawberry cake
For our dinner to-day.

Roger:

      For dear principle's sake
I could easily do what you ask, were it not
Most unkind to Miss Ruth, who gave labor and thought
To that menu, preparing it quite to my taste.

Ruth:

But the thought and the dinner will both go to waste,
If we linger here longer; and Mabel, I see,
Is impatient to go to her duties.

Roger:

      The bee
Is reluctant to turn from the lily although
The lily may obviously wish he would go
And leave her to muse in the sunlight alone.
Yet when the rose calls him, his sorrow, I own,
Has its recompense. So from delight to delight
I fly with my wings honeyladen.

Good night.

Oh, love is like the dawnlight
  That turns the dark to day,
And love is like the deep night
  With secrets hid away.

And love is like the moonlight
  Where tropic Summers glow,
And love is like the twilight
  When dreams begin to grow.

Oh, love is like the sunlight
  That sets the world ablaze.
And love is like the moonlight
  With soft illusive rays.

And love is like the starlight
  That glimmers o'er the skies.
And love is like the far light
  That shines from God's great eyes.

III.

Maurice Somerville from his turreted den
Looked out of the window and laid down his pen.
A soft salty wind from the water was blowing,
Below in the garden sat Ruth with her sewing.
And stretched on the grass at her feet Roger lay
With a book in his hand.

      Through the ripe August day,
Piped the Katydids' voices, Jack Frost's tally-ho
Commanding Queen Summer to pack up and go.
Maurice leaned his head on the casement and sighed,
Strong and full in his heart surged love's turbulent tide.
And thoughts of the woman he worshiped with longing
Took shape and like angels about him came thronging.
The world was all Mabel! her exquisite face
Seemed etched on the sunlight and gave it its grace;
Her eyes made the blue of the heavens, the sun
Was her wonderful hair caught and coiled into one
Shining mass. With a reverent, worshipful awe,
It was Mabel, fair Mabel, dear Mabel he saw,
When he looked up to God.

      They had been much together
Through all the bright stretches of midsummer weather,
Ruth, Roger, and Mabel and he. Scarce a day
But the four were united in work or in play.
And much of the play to a man or a maid
Not in love had seemed labor. Recital, charade,

Garden party, church festival, musical, hop,
Were all planned by Miss Lee without respite or stop.
The poor were the richer; school, hospital, church,
The heathen, the laborer left in the lurch
By misfortune, the orphan, the indigent old,
Our kind Lady Bountiful aided with gold
Which she filched from the pockets of pleasure--God's spoil,
And God's blessing will follow such lives when they toil
Through an infinite sympathy.

      Fair Mabel Lee
Loved to rule and to lead. She was eager to be
In the eyes of the public. That modern day craze
Possessed her in secret, and this was its phase.
An innocent, even commendable, fad
Which filled empty larders and cheered up the sad.
She loved to do good. But, alas! in her heart,
She loved better still the authoritative part
Which she played in her town.

      'Neath the saint's aureole
Lurked the feminine tyrant who longed to control,
And who never would serve; but her sway was so sweet,
That her world was contented to bow at her feet.

Who toils in the great public vineyard must needs
Let other hands keep his own garden from weeds.
So busy was Mabel with charity fairs
She gave little thought to her home or its cares.
Mrs. Lee, like the typical modern day mother,
Was maid to her daughter; the father and brother
Were slaves at her bidding; an excellent plan
To make a tyrannical wife for some man.

Yet where was the man who, beholding the grace
Of that slight girlish creature, and watching her face
With its infantile beauty and sweetness, would dare
Think aught but the rarest of virtues dwelt there?
Rare virtues she had, but in commonplace ones
Which make happy husbands and home loving sons
She was utterly lacking. Ruth Somerville saw
In sorrow and silence this blemishing flaw
In the friend whom she loved with devotion! Maurice
Saw only the angel with eyes full of peace.
The faults of plain women are easily seen.
But who cares to peer back of beauty's fair screen
For things which are ugly to look on?

      The lover
Is not quite in love when his sharp eyes discover
The flaws in his jewel.

      Maurice from his room
Looked dreamily down on the garden of bloom,
Where Ruth sat with Roger; he smiled as he thought
How quickly the world sated cynic was brought
Into harness by Cupid. The man mad with drink,
And the man mad with love, is quite certain to think
All other men drunkards or lovers. In truth
Maurice had expected his friend to love Ruth.
"She was young, she was fair; with her bright sunny art
She could scatter the mists from his world befogged heart.
She could give him the one heaven under God's dome,
A peaceful, well ordered, and love-guarded home.
And he? why of course he would worship her! When
Cupid finds the soft spot in the hearts of such men
They are ideal husbands." Maurice Somerville

Felt the whole world was shaping itself to his will.
And his heart stirred with joy as, by thought necromancy,
He made the near future unfold to his fancy,
And saw Ruth the bride of his friend, and the place
She left vacant supplied with the beauty and grace
Of this woman he longed for, the love of his life,
Fair Mabel, his angel, his sweet spirit wife.

Maurice to his desk turned again and once more
Began to unburden his bosom and pour
His heart out on paper--the poet's relief,
When drunk with life's rapture or sick with its grief.

Song.

When shall I tell my lady that I love her?
  Will it be while the sunshine woos the world,
Or when the mystic twilight bends above her,
  Or when the day's bright banners all are furled?
Will wild winds shriek, or will the calm stars glow,
When I shall tell her that I love her so,
        I love her so?

I think the sun should shine in all his glory;
  Again, the twilight seems the fitting time.
Yet sweet dark night would understand the story,
  So old, so new, so tender, so sublime.
Wild storms should rage to chord with my desire,
Yet faithful stars should shine and never tire,
        And never tire.

Ah, if my lady will consent to listen,
  All hours, all times, shall hear my story told.
In amorous dawns, on nights when pale stars glisten
  In dim hushed gloamings and in noon hours bold,
While thunders crash, and while the winds breathe low,
Will I re-tell her that I love her so.
        I love her so.

IV.

The October day had been luscious and fair
Like a woman of thirty. A chill in the air
As the sun faced the west spoke of frost lurking near.
All day the Sound lay without motion, and clear
As a mirror, and blue as a blond baby's eyes.
A change in the tide brought a change to the skies.
The bay stirred and murmured and parted its lips
And breathed a long sigh for the lost lovely ships,
That had gone with the Summer.

        Its calm placid breast
Was stirred into passionate pain and unrest.
Not a sail, not a sail anywhere to be seen!
The soft azure eyes of the sea turned to green.
A sudden wind rose; like a runaway horse
Unchecked and unguided it sped on its course.
The waves bared their teeth, and spat spray in the face

Of the furious gale as they fled in the chase.
The sun hurried into a cloud; and the trees
Bowed low and yet lower, as if to appease
The wrath of the storm king that threatened them. Close
To the waves at their wildest stood Roger Montrose.
The day had oppressed him; and now the unrest
Of the wind beaten sea brought relief to his breast,
Or at least brought the sense of companionship. Lashed
By his higher emotions, the man's passions dashed
On the shore of his mind in a frenzy of pain,
Like the waves on the rocks, and a frenzy as vain.

Since the day he first looked on her face, Mabel Lee
Had seemed to his self sated nature to be,
On life's troubled ocean, a beacon of light,
To guide him safe out from the rocks and the night.
Her calm soothed his passion; her peace gave him poise;
She seemed like a silence in life's vulgar noise.
He bathed in the light which her purity cast,
And felt half absolved from the sins of the past.
He longed in her mantle of goodness to hide
And forget the whole world. By the incoming tide
He talked with his heart as one talks with a friend
Who is dying. "The summer has come to an end
And I wake from my dreaming," he mused. "Wake to know
That my place is not here--I must go--I must go.
Who dares laugh at Love shall hear Love laughing last,
As forth from his bowstring barbed arrows are cast.
I scoffed at the god with a sneer on my lip,
And he forces me now from his chalice to sip
A bitter sweet potion. Ah, lightly the part
Of a lover I've played many times, but my heart
Has been proud in its record of friendship. And now

The mad, eager lover born in me must bow
To the strong claims of friendship. I love Mabel Lee;
Dared I woo as I would, I could make her love me.
The soul of a maid who knows not passion's fire
Is moth to the flame of a man's strong desire.
With one kiss on her lips I could banish the nun
And wake in her virginal bosom the one
Mighty love of her life. If I leave her, I know
She will be my friend's wife in a season or so.
He loves her, he always has loved her; 'tis he
Who ever will do all the loving; and she
Will accept it, and still be the saint to the end,
And she never will know what she missed; but my friend
Has the right to speak first. God! how can he delay?
I marvel at men who are fashioned that way.
He has worshiped her since first she put up her tresses,
And let down the hem of her school-girlish dresses
And now she is full twenty-two; were I he
A brood of her children should climb on my knee
By this time! What a sin against love to postpone
The day that might make her forever his own.
The man who can wait has no blood in his veins.
Maurice is a dreamer, he loves with his brains
Not with soul and with senses. And yet his whole life
Will be blank if he makes not this woman his wife.
She is woof of his dreams, she is warp of his mind;
Who tears her away shall leave nothing behind.
No, no, I am going: farewell to Bay Bend
I am no woman's lover--I *am* one man's friend.
Still-born in the arms of the matron eyed year
Lies the beautiful dream that my life buries here.
Its tomb was its cradle; it came but to taunt me,
It died, but its phantom shall ever more haunt me."

He turned from the waves that leaped at him in wrath
To find Mabel Lee, like a wraith, in his path.
The rose from her cheek had departed in fear;
The tip of her eyelash was gemmed with a tear.
The rude winds had disarranged mantle and dress,
And she clung with both hands to her hat in distress.
"I am frightened," she cried, in a tremulous tone;
"I dare not proceed any farther alone.
As I came by the church yard the wind felled a tree,
And invisible hands seemed to hurl it at me;
I hurried on, shrieking; the wind, in disgust,
Tore the hat from my head, filled my eyes full of dust,
And otherwise made me the butt of its sport.
Just then I spied you, like a light in the port,
And I steered for you. Please do not laugh at my fright!
I am really quite bold in the calm and the light,
But when a storm gathers, or darkness prevails,
My courage deserts me, my bravery fails,
And I want to hide somewhere and cover my ears,
And give myself up to weak womanish tears."

Her ripple of talk allowed Roger Montrose
A few needed moments to calm and compose
His excited emotions; to curb and control
The turbulent feelings that surged through his soul
At the sudden encounter.

      "I quite understand,"
He said in a voice that was under command
Of his will, "All your fears in a storm of this kind.
There is something uncanny and weird in the wind;
Intangible, viewless, it speeds on its course,

And forests and oceans must yield to its force.
What art has constructed with patience and toil,
The wind in one second of time can despoil.
It carries destruction and death and despair,
Yet no man can follow it into its lair
And bind it or stay it--this thing without form.
Ah! there comes the rain! we are caught in the storm.
Put my coat on your shoulders and come with me where
Yon rock makes a shelter--I often sit there
To watch the great conflicts 'twixt tempest and sea.
Let me lie at your feet! 'Tis the last time, Miss Lee,
I shall see you, perchance, in this life, who can say?
I leave on the morrow at break o' the day."

Mabel:

Indeed? Why, how sudden! and may I inquire
The reason you leave us without one desire
To return? for your words seem a final adieu.

Roger:

I never expect to return, that is true,
Yet my wish is to stay.

Mabel:

Are you not your own master?

Roger:

Alas, yes! and therein lies the cause of disaster.
Myself bids me go, my calm, reasoning part,

The will is the man, not the poor, foolish heart,
Which is ever at war with the intellect. So
I silence its clamoring voices and go.
Were I less my own master, I then might remain.

Mabel:

Your words are but riddles, I beg you explain.

Roger:

No, no, rather bid me keep silent! To say
Why I go were as weak on my part as to stay.

Mabel:

I think you most cruel! You know, sir, my sex
Loves dearly a secret. Then why should you vex
And torment me in this way by hinting at one?

Roger:

Let us talk of the weather, I think the storm done.

Mabel:

Very well! I will go! No, you need not come too,
And I will not shake hands, I am angry with you.

Roger:

And you will not shake hands when we part for all time?

Mabel:

Then read me your riddle!

Roger:

      No, that were a crime
Against honor and friendship; girl, girl, have a care--
You are goading my poor, tortured heart to despair.

His last words were lost in the loud thunder's crash;
The sea seemed ablaze with a sulphurous flash.
From the rocks just above them an evergreen tree
Was torn up by the roots and flung into the sea.
The waves with rude arms hurled it back on the shore;
The wind gained in fury. The glare and the roar
Of the lightning and tempest paled Mabel Lee's cheek,
Her pupils dilated; she sprang with a shriek
Of a terrified child lost to all save alarm,
And clasped Roger Montrose with both hands by the arm,
While her cheek pressed his shoulder. An agony, sweet
And unbearable, thrilled from his head to his feet,
His veins were like rivers, with billows of fire:
His will lost control; and long fettered desire
Slipped its leash. He caught Mabel Lee to his breast,
Drew her face up to his, on her frightened lips pressed
Wild caresses of passion that startled and shocked.
Like a madman he looked, like a madman he talked,
Waiting not for reply, with no pause but a kiss,
While his iron arms welded her bosom to his.
"Girl, girl, you demanded my secret," he cried;
"Well, that bruise on your lips tells the story! I tried,
Good God, how I tried! to be silent and go

Without speaking one word, without letting you know
That I loved you; yet how could you look in my eyes
And not see love was there like the sun in the skies?
Ah, those hands on my arm--that dear head lightly pressed
On my shoulder! God, woman, the heart in my breast
Was dry powder, your touch was the spark; and the blame
Must be yours if both lives are scorched black with the flame.
Do you hate me, despise me, for being so weak?
No, no! let me kiss you again ere you speak!
You are mine for the moment; and mine--mine alone
Is the first taste of passion your soft mouth has known.
Whoever forestalls me in winning your hand,
Between you and him shall this mad moment stand--
You shall think of me, though you think only to hate.
There--speak to me--speak to me--tell me my fate;
On your words, Mabel Lee, hangs my whole future life.
I covet you, covet you, sweet, for my wife;
I want to stay here at your side. Since I first
Saw your face I have felt an unquenchable thirst
To be good--to look deep in your eyes and find God,
And to leave in the past the dark paths I have trod
In my search after pleasure. Ah, must I go back
Into folly again, to retread the old track
Which leads out into nothingness? Girl, answer me,
As souls answer at Judgment."

      The face of the sea
Shone with sudden pink splendor. The riotous wind
Swooned away with exhaustion. Each dark cloud seemed lined
With vermilion. The tempest was over. A word
Floated up like a feather; the silence was stirred
By the soul of a sigh. The last remnant of gray
In the skies turned to gold, as a voice whispered, "Stay."

God grinds His poor people to powder
  All day and all night I can hear,
Their cries growing louder and louder.
  Oh, God, have You deadened Your ear?

The chimes in old Trinity steeple
  Ring in the sweet season of prayer,
And still God is grinding His people,
  He is grinding them down to despair.

Mind, body and muscle and marrow,
  He grinds them again and again.
Can He who takes heed of the sparrow
  Be blind to the tortures of men?

V.

In a bare little room of a tenement row
Of the city, Maurice sat alone. It was so
(In this nearness to life's darkest phases of grief
And despair) that his own bitter woe found relief.
Joy needs no companion; but sorrow and pain
Long to comrade with sorrow. The flowery chain
Flung by Pleasure about her gay votaries breaks
With the least strain upon it. The chain sorrow makes
Links heart unto heart. As a bullock will fly

To far fields when an arrow has pierced him, to die,
So Maurice had flown over far oceans to find
No balm for his wounds, and no peace for his mind.
Cosmopolitan, always, is sorrow; at home
In all countries and lands, thriving well while we roam
In vain efforts to slay it. Toil only, brings peace
To the tempest tossed heart. What in travel Maurice
Failed to find--self-forgetfulness--came with his work
For the suffering poor in the slums of New York.

He had wandered in strange heathen countries--had been
Among barbarous hordes; but the greed and the sin
Of his own native land seemed the shame of the hour.
In his gold there was balm, in his pen there was power
To comfort the needy, to aid and defend
The unfortunate. Close in their midst, as a friend
And companion, for more than twelve months he had dwelt.
Like a ray of pure light in a cellar was felt
This strong, wholesome presence. His little room bare
Of all luxuries, taught the poor souls who flocked there
For his counsel and aid, how by mere cleanliness
The grim features of want lose some lines of distress.
The slips from the plants on his window ledge, given
To beauty starved souls, spoke more clearly of heaven
And God than did sermons or dry creedy tracts.
Maurice was no preacher; and yet his kind acts
Of mercy and self-immolation sufficed
To wake in dark minds a bright image of Christ--
The Christ often heard of, but doubted before.
Maurice spoke no word of religion. Of yore
His heart had accepted the creeds of his youth
Without pausing to cavil, or question their truth.
Faith seemed his inheritance. But, with the blow

Which slew love and killed friendship, faith, too, seemed to go.

It is easy to be optimistic in pleasure,
But when Pain stands us up by her portal to measure
The actual height of our trust and belief,
Ah! then is the time when our faith comes to grief.
The woes of our fellows, God sends them, 'tis plain;
But the devil himself is the cause of *our* pain.
We question the wisdom that rules o'er the world,
And our minds into chaos and darkness are hurled.

The average scoffer at faith goes about
Pouring into the ears of his fellows each doubt
Which assails him. One truth he fails wholly to heed;
That a doubt oft repeated may bore like a creed.

Maurice kept his thoughts to himself, but his pen
Was dipped in the gall of his heart now and then,
And his muse was the mouthpiece. The sin unforgiven
I hold by the Cherubim chanting in heaven
Is the sin of the poet who dares sing a strain
Which adds to the world's awful chorus of pain
And repinings. The souls whom the gods bless at birth
With the great gift of song, have been sent to the earth
To better and brighten it. Woe to the heart
Which lets its own sorrow embitter its art.
Unto him shall more sorrow be given; and life
After life filled with sorrow, till, spent with the strife,
He shall cease from rebellion, and bow to the rod
In submission, and own and acknowledge his God.

Maurice, with his unwilling muse in the gloom
Of a mood pessimistic, was shut in his room.

A whistle, a step on the stairway, a knock,
Then over the transom there fluttered a flock
Of white letters. The Muse, with a sigh of content,
Left the poet to read them, and hurriedly went
Back to pleasanter regions. Maurice glanced them through:
There were brief business epistles from two
Daily papers, soliciting work from his pen;
A woman begged money for Christ's sake; three men
Asked employment; a mother wrote only to say
How she blessed him and prayed God to bless him each day
For his kindness to her and to hers; and the last
Was a letter from Ruth. The pale ghost of the past
Rose out of its poor shallow grave, with the scent
And the mold of the clay clinging to it, and leant
O'er Maurice as he read, while its breath fanned his cheek.

"Forgive me," wrote Ruth; "for at last I must speak
Of the two whom you wish to forget. Well I know
How you suffered, still suffer, from fate's sudden blow,
Though I am a woman, and women must stay
And fight out pain's battles where men run away.
But my strength has its limit, my courage its end,
The time has now come when I, too, leave Bay Bend.
Maurice, let the bitterness housed in your heart
For the man you long loved as a comrade, depart,
And let pity replace it. Oh, weep for his sorrow--
From your fountain of grief, held in check, let me borrow;
I have so overdrawn on the bank of my tears
That my anguish is now refused payment. For years
You loved Mabel Lee. Well, to some hearts love speaks
His whole tale of passion in brief little weeks.
As Minerva, full grown, from the great brow of Jove
Sprang to life, so full blown from our breasts may spring Love.

Love hid like a bee in my heart's lily cup;
I knew not he was there till his sting woke me up.

Maurice, oh Maurice! Can you fancy the woe
Of seeing the prize which you coveted so
Misused, or abused, by another? The wife
Of the man whom I worshiped is spoiling the life
That was wax in her hands, wax to shape as she chose.
You were blind to her faults, so was Roger Montrose.
Both saw but the saint; well, let saints keep their places,
And not crowd the women in life's hurried races.
As saint, Mabel Lee might succeed; but, oh brother,
She never was meant for a wife or a mother.
Her beautiful home has the desolate air
Of a house that is ruled by its servants. The care--
The thought of the *woman* (that sweet, subtle power
Pervading some rooms like the scent of a flower),
Which turns house into home--that is lacking. She goes
On her merciful rounds, does our Lady Montrose,
Looking after the souls of the heathen, and leaving
The poor hungry soul of her lord to its grieving.

He craves her companionship; wants her to be
At his side, more his own, than the public's. But she
Holds such love is but selfish; and thinks he should make
Some sacrifice gladly for charity's sake.
Her schools, and her clubs, and her fairs fill her time;
He wants her to travel; no, that were a crime
To go seeking for pleasure, and leave duty here.
God had given her work and her labor lay near.
A month of the theater season in town?
No, the stage is an evil that needs putting down
By good people. So, scheme as he will, the poor man

Has to finally yield every project and plan
To this sweet stubborn saint; for the husband, you see,
Stands last in Her thoughts. He has come, after three
Patient years, to that knowledge; his wishes, his needs
Must always give way to her whims, or her creeds.

She knows not the primer of loving; her soul
Is engrossed with the poor petty wish to ***control***.
And she chafes at restriction. Love loves to be bound,
And its sweetest of freedom in bondage is found.
She pulls at her fetters. One worshiping heart
And its faithful devotion play but a small part
In her life. She would rather be lauded and praised
By a crowd of inferior followers, raised
To the pitiful height of their leader, than be
One man's goddess. There, now, is the true Mabel Lee!
Grieve not that you lost her, but grieve for the one
Who with me stood last night by the corpse of his son,
And with me stood alone. Ah! how wisely and well
Could Mabel descant on Maternity! tell
Other women the way to train children to be
An honor and pride to their parents! Yet she,
From the first, left her child to the nurses. She found
'Twas a tax on her nerves to have baby around
When it worried and cried. The nurse knew what to do,
And a block down the street lived Mama! 'twixt the two
Little Roger would surely be cared for. She must
Keep her strength and be worthy the love and the trust
Of the poor, who were yearly increasing, and not
Bestow on her own all the care and the thought--
That were selfishness, surely.

Well, the babe grew apace,
But yesterday morning a flush on its face
And a look in its eye worried Roger. The mother
Was due at some sort of convention or other
In Boston--I think 'twas a grand federation
Of clubs formed by women to rescue the Nation
From man's awful clutches; and Mabel was made
The head delegate of the Bay Bend Brigade.
Once drop in a small, selfish nature the seed
Of ambition for place, and it grows like a weed.
The fair village angel we called Mabel Lee,
As Mrs. Montrose, has developed, you see,
To a full fledged Reformer. It quite turned her head
To be sent to the city of beans and brown bread
As a delegate! (Delegate! magical word!
The heart of the queer modern woman is stirred
Far more by its sound than by aught she may hear
In the phrases poor Cupid pours into her ear.)
Mabel chirped to the baby a dozen good-byes,
And laughed at the trouble in Roger's grave eyes,
As she leaned o'er the lace ruffled crib of her son
And talked baby-talk: "Now be good, 'ittle one,
While Mama is away, and don't draw a long breath,
Unless 'oo would worry Papa half to death.
And don't cough, and, of all things, don't *sneeze*, 'ittle dear,
Or Papa will be thrown into spasms of fear.
Now, good-bye, once again, 'ittle man; mother knows
There is no other baby like Roger Montrose
In the whole world to-day."

So she left him. That night
The nurse sent a messenger speeding in fright
For the Doctor; a second for Grandmama Lee

And Roger despatched still another for me.
All in vain! through the gray chilly paths of the dawn
The soul of the beautiful baby passed on
Into Mother-filled lands.

       Ah! my God, the despair
Of seeing that agonized sufferer there;
To stand by his side, yet denied the relief
Of sharing, as wife, and as mother, his grief.
Enough! I have borne all I can bear. The role
Of friend to a lover pulls hard on the soul
Of a sensitive woman. The three words in life
Which have meaning to me are home, mother and wife--
Or, rather, wife, mother and home. Once I thought
Men cared for the women who found home the spot
Next to heaven for happiness; women who knew
No ambition beyond being loyal and true,
And who loved all the tasks of the housewife. I learn,
Instead, that from women of that kind men turn,
With a yawn, unto those who are useless; who live
For the poor hollow world and for what it can give,
And who make home the spot where, when other joys cease,
One sleeps late when one wishes.

      You left me Maurice
Left the home I have kept since our dear Mother died,
With such sisterly love and such housewifely pride,
And you wandered afar, and for what cause, forsooth?
Oh! because a vain, self-loving woman, in truth,
Had been faithless. The man whom I worshiped, ignored
The love and the ***comfort*** my woman's heart stored
In its depths for his taking, and sought Mabel Lee.
Well, I'm done with the role of the housewife. I see

There is nothing in being domestic. The part
Is unpicturesque, and at war with all art.
The senile old Century leers with dim eyes
At our sex and demands that we shock or surprise
His thin blood into motion. The home's not the place
To bring a pleased smile to his wicked old face.
To the mandate I bow; since all strive for that end,
I must join the great throng! I am leaving Bay Bend
This day week. I will see you in town as I pass
To the college at C----, where I enter the class
Of medical students--I fancy you will
Like to see my name thus--Dr. Ruth Somerville."

Maurice dropped the long, closely written epistle,
Stared hard at the wall, and gave vent to a whistle.
A Doctor! his sweet, little home-loving sister.
A Doctor! one might as well prefix a Mister
To Ruth Somerville, that most feminine name.
And then in the wake of astonishment came
Keen pity for all she had suffered. "Poor Ruth,
She writes like an agonized woman, in truth,
And like one torn with jealousy. Ah, I can see,"
He mused, "how the pure soul of sweet Mabel Lee
Revolts at the bondage and shrinks from the ban
That lies in the love of that sensual man.
He is of the earth, earthy. He loves but her beauty,
He cares not for conscience, or honor or duty.
Like a moth she was dazzled and lured by the flame
Of a light she thought love, till she learned its true name;
When she found it mere passion, it lost all its charms.
No wonder she flies from his fettering arms!
God pity you, Mabel! poor ill mated wife;
But my love, like a planet, shall watch o'er your life,

Though all other light from your skies disappear,
Like a sun in the darkness my love shall appear.
Unselfish and silent, it asks no return,
But while the great firmament lasts it shall burn."

Muse, muse, awake, and sing thy loneliest strain,
Song, song, be sad with sorrow's deepest pain,
Heart, heart, bow down and never bound again,
      My Lady grieves, she grieves.

Night, night, draw close thy filmy mourning veil,
Moon, moon, conceal thy beauty sweet and pale,
Wind, wind, sigh out thy most pathetic wail,
      My Lady grieves, she grieves.

Time, time, speed by, thou art too slow, too slow,
Grief, grief, pass on, and take thy cup of woe,
Life, life, be kind, ah! do not wound her so,
      My Lady grieves, she grieves.

Sleep, sleep, dare not to touch mine aching eyes,
Love, love, watch on, though fate thy wish denies,
Heart, heart, sigh on, since she, my Lady, sighs,
      My Lady grieves, she grieves.

The flower breathes low to the bee,
  "Behold, I am ripe with bloom.
Let Love have his way with me,
  Ere I fall unwed in my tomb."

The rooted plant sighs in distress

To the winds by the garden walk
"Oh, waft me my lover's caress,
  Or I shrivel and die on my stalk."

The whippoorwill utters her love
  In a passionate "Come, oh come,"
To the male in the depths of the grove,
  But the heart of a woman is dumb.

The lioness seeks her mate,
  The she-tiger calls her own--
Who made it a woman's fate
  To sit in the silence alone?

VI.

Wooed, wedded and widowed ere twenty. The life
Of Zoe Travers is told in that sentence. A wife
For one year, loved and loving; so full of life's joy
That death, growing jealous, resolved to destroy
The Eden she dwelt in. Five desolate years
She walked robed in weeds, and bathed ever in tears,
Through the valley of memory. Locked in love's tomb
Lay youth in its glory and hope in its bloom.
At times she was filled with religious devotion,
Again crushed to earth with rebellious emotion

And unresigned sorrow.

   Ah, wild was her grief!
And the years seemed to bring her no balm of relief.
When a heart from its sorrow time cannot estrange,
God sends it another to alter and change
The current of feeling. Zoe's mother, her one
Tie to earth, became ill. When the doctors had done
All the harm which they dared do with powder and pill,
They ordered a trial of Dame Nature's skill.
Dear Nature! what grief in her bosom must stir
When she sees us turn everywhere save unto her
For the health she holds always in keeping; and sees
Us at last, when too late, creeping back to her knees,
Begging that she at first could have given!

   'Twas so
Mother Nature's heart grieved o'er the mother of Zoe,
Who came but to die on her bosom. She died
Where the mocking bird poured out its passionate tide
Of lush music; and all through the dark days of pain
That succeeded, and over and through the refrain
Of her sorrow, Zoe heard that wild song evermore.
It seemed like a blow which pushed open a door
In her heart. Something strange, sweet and terrible stirred
In her nature, aroused by the song of that bird.
It rang like a voice from the future; a call
That came not from the past; yet the past held her all.
To the past she had plighted her vows; in the past
Lay her one dream of happiness, first, only, last.

Alone in the world now, she felt the unrest
Of an unanchored boat on the wild billow's breast.

Two homes had been shattered; the West held but tombs.
She drifted again where the magnolia blooms
And the mocking bird sings. Oh! that song, that wild strain,
Whose echoes still haunted her heart and her brain!
How she listened to hear it repeated! It came
Through the dawn to her heart, and the sound was like flame.
It chased all the shadows of night from her room,
And burst the closed bud of the day into bloom.
It leaped to the heavens, it sank to the earth
It gave life new rapture and love a new birth.
It ran through her veins like a fiery stream,
And the past and its sorrow--was only a dream.

The call of a bird in the spring for its lover
Is the voice of all Nature when winter is over.
The heart of the woman re-echoed the strain,
And its meaning, at last, to her senses was plain.

Grief's winter was over, the snows from her heart
Were melted; hope's blossoms were ready to start.
The spring had returned with its siren delights,
And her youth and emotions asserted their rights.
Then memory struggled with passion. The dead
Seemed to rise from the grave and accuse her. She fled
From her thoughts as from lepers; returned to old ways,
And strove to keep occupied, filling her days
With devotional duties. But when the night came
She heard through her slumber that song like a flame,
And her dreams were sweet torture. She sought all too soon
To chill the warm sun of her youth's ardent noon
With the shadows of premature evening. Her mind
Lacked direction and purpose. She tried in a blind,
Groping fashion to follow an early ideal

Of love and of constancy, starving the real
Affectional nature God gave her. She prayed
For God's help in unmaking the woman He made,
As if He repented the thing He had done.
With the soul of a Sappho, she lived like a nun,
Hid her thoughts from all women, from men kept apart,
And carefully guarded the book of her heart
From the world's prying eyes. Yet men read through the cover,
And knew that the story was food for a lover.
(The dullest of men seemed possessed of the art
To read what the passions inscribe on the heart.
Though written in cipher and sealed from the sight,
Yet masculine eyes will interpret aright.)
Worn out with the unceasing conflict at last,
Zoe fled from herself and her sorrowful past,
And turned to new scenes for diversion from thought.

New York! oh, what magic encircles that spot
In the feminine mind of the West! There, it seems,
Waits the realization of beautiful dreams.
There the waters of Lethe unceasingly roll,
With blessed forgetfulness free to each soul,
While the doorways that lead to success open wide,
With Fame in the distance to beckon and guide.
Mirth lurks in each byway, and Folly herself
Wears the look of a semi-respectable elf,
And is to be courted and trusted when met,
For she teaches one how to be gay and forget,
And to start new account books with life.

        It was so,
Since she first heard the name of the city, that Zoe
Dreamed of life in New York. It was thither she turned

To smother the heart that with restlessness burned,
And to quiet and calm an unsatisfied mind.
Her plans were but outlines, crude, vague, undefined,
Of distraction and pleasure. A snug little home,
With seclusion and comfort; full freedom to roam
Where her fancy and income permitted; new faces,
New scenes, new environments, far from the places
Where brief joy and long sorrow had dwelt with her; free
From the curious eyes that seemed ever to be
Bent upon her. She passed like a ship from the port,
Without chart or compass; the plaything and sport
Of the billows of Fate.

    The parks were all gay
And busy with costuming duties of May
When Zoe reached New York. The rain and the breeze
Had freshened the gowns of the Northern pine trees
Till they looked bright as new; all the willows were seen
In soft dainty garments of exquisite green.
Young buds swelled with life, and reached out to invite
And to hold the warm gaze of the wandering light.
The turf exhaled fragrance; among the green boughs
The unabashed city birds plighted their vows,
Or happy young house hunters chirped of the best
And most suitable nook to establish a nest.

There was love in the sunshine, and love in the air;
Youth, hope, home, companionship, spring, everywhere.
There was youth, there was spring in her blood; yet she only,
In all the great city, seemed loveless and lonely.

The trim little flat, facing north on the park,
Was not homelike; the rooms seemed too sombre and dark

To her eyes, sun-accustomed; the neighbors too near
And too noisy. The medley of sounds hurt her ear.
Sudden laughter; the cry of an infant; the splash
Of a tenant below in his bath-tub; the crash
Of strong hands on a keyboard above, and the light,
Merry voice of the lady who lived opposite,
The air intertwined in a tangled sound ball,
And flung straight at her ear through the court and the hall.

Ah, what loneliness dwelt in the rush and the stir
Of the great pushing throngs that were nothing to her,
And to whom she was nothing! Her heart, on its quest
For distraction, seemed eating itself in her breast.
She longed for a comrade, a friend. In the church
Which she frequented no one abetted her search,
For the faces of people she met in its aisle
Gazed calmly beyond her, without glance or smile.
The look in their eyes, when translated, read thus,
"We worship God here, what are people to us?"
In some masculine eyes she read more, it is true.
What she read made her gaze at the floor of her pew.

The blithe little blonde who lived over the hall,
In the opposite rooms, was the first one to call
Or to show friendly feeling. She seemed sweet and kind,
But her infantile face hid a mercantile mind.
Her voice had the timbre of metal. Each word
Clinked each word like small change in a purse; and you heard,
In the rustling silk of her skirts, just a hint
Of new bills freshly printed and right from the mint.

There was that in her airs and her chatter which made
Zoe question and ponder, and turn half afraid

From her proffers of friendship. When one July day
The fair neighbor called for a moment to say,
"I am off to Long Branch for the summer, good-bye,"
Zoe seemed to breathe freer--she scarcely knew why,
But she reasoned it out as alone in the gloom
Of the soft summer evening she sat in her room.
"The woman is happy," she said; "at the least,
Her heart is not starving in life's ample feast.
She lives while she lives, but I only exist,
And Fate laughs in my face for the things I resist."

New York in the midsummer seems like the gay
Upper servant who rules with the mistress away.
She entertains friends from all parts of the earth;
Her streets are alive with a fictitious mirth.
She flaunts her best clothes with a devil-may-care
Sort of look, and her parks wear a riotous air.
There is something unwholesome about her at dusk;
Her trees, and her gardens, seem scented with musk;
And you feel she has locked up the door of the house
And, half drunk with the heat, wanders forth to carouse,
With virtue, ambition and industry all
Packed off (moth-protected) with garments for Fall.

Zoe felt out of step with the town. In the song
Which it sang, where each note was a soul of the throng,
She seemed the one discord. Books gave no distraction.
She cared not for study, her heart longed for action,
For pleasure, excitement. Wild impulses, new
To her mind, came like demons and urged her to do
All sorts of mad things. Mischief breathed through the air.
One could do as one liked in New York--who would care--
Who would know save the God who had left her alone

In his world, unprotected, unloved? From her own
Restless mind and sick heart she attempted once more
To escape. One reads much of gay life at the shore--
Narragansett, she fancied, would suit her. The sea
Would at least prove a friend; and, perchance, there might be
Some heart, like her own, seeking comradeship there.
The days brought no friend. But the moist, salty air
Was a stimulant, giving existence new charms.
The sea was a lover who opened his arms
Every day to embrace her. And life in this place
Held something of pleasure, and sweetness and grace,
Though the eyes of the men were too ardent and bold,
And the eyes of the women suspicious and cold,
She yet had the sea--the sea, strong and mighty,
Both father and mother of fair Aphrodite.

VII.

Mabel grieved for her child with a sorrow sincere,
But she bowed to the will of her Maker. No tear
Came to soften the hard, stony look in the eye
Of her husband; she heard no complaint and no sigh
From his lips, but he turned with impatience whenever
She spoke of religion, or made one endeavor
To lead his thoughts up from the newly turned sod
Where the little form slept, to its spirit with God.

Long hours by that grave, Roger passed, and alone.
The woes of her neighbors his wife made her own,
But her husband she pointed to Christ; and in grief
Prayed for light to be cast on his dark unbelief.

She flung herself into good works more and more,
And saw not that the look which her husband's face wore
Was the look of a man starved for love. In the mold
Of a nun she was fashioned, chaste, passionless, cold.
(Such women sin more when they take marriage ties
Than the love-maddened creature who lawlessly lies
In the arms of the man whom she worships. The child
Not conceived in true love leaves the mother defiled.
Though an army of clergymen sanction her vows,
God sees "illegitimate" stamped on the brows
Of her offspring. Love only can legalize birth
In His eyes--all the rest is but spawn of the earth.)

Mabel Lee, as the maid, had been flattered and pleased
By the passion of Roger; his wild wooing teased
That inquisitive sense, half a fault, half a merit,
Which the daughters of Eve, to a woman, inherit.
His love fanned her love for herself to a glow;
She was stirred by the thought she could stir a man so.
That was all. She had nothing to give in return.
One can't light a fire with no fuel to burn;
And the love Roger dreamed he could rouse in her soul
Was not there to be wakened. He stood at his goal
As the Arctic explorer may finally stand,
To see all about him an ice prisoned land,
White, beautiful, useless.

Some women are chaste,
Like the snows which envelop the bleak arid waste
Of the desert; once melted, alas! what remains
But the poor, unproductive, dry soil of the plains?
The flora of Cupid will never be found,
However he toil there, to thrive in such ground.

Mabel Montrose was held in the highest esteem
By her neighbors; I think neighbors everywhere deem
Such women to be all that's noble. They sighed
When they spoke of her husband; they told how she tried
To convert him, and how they had thought for a season
His mind was bent Christ-ward; and then, with no reason,
He seemed to drift back to the world, and grew jealous
Of Mabel, and thought her too faithful and zealous
In duty to others.

The death of his child
Only hardened his heart against God. He grew wild,
Took to drink; spent a week at a time in the city,
Neglecting his saint of a wife--such a pity.
It was true. Our friends keep a sharp eye on our deeds
But the fine interlining of causes--who heeds?
The long list of heartaches which lead to rash acts
Would bring pity, not blame, if the world knew the facts.

There are women so terribly free from all evil,
They discourage a man, and he goes to the devil.
There are people whose virtues result in appalling,
And they prove a great aid to his majesty's calling.

Roger's wife rendered goodness so dreary and cold,
His tendril-like will lost its poor little hold

On the new better life he was longing to reach,
And slipped back to the dust. Oh! to love, not to preach.
Is a woman's true method of helping mankind.
The sinner is won through his heart, not his mind.
As the sun loves the seed up to life through the sod,
So the patience of love brings a soul to its God.
But when love is lacking, the devil is sure
To stand in the pathway with some sort of lure.
Roger turned to the world for distraction. The world
Smiled a welcome, and then like an octopus curled
All its tentacles 'round him, and dragged him away
Into deep, troubled waters.

      One late summer day
He awoke with a headache, which will not surprise,
When you know that his bedtime had been at sunrise,
And that gay Narraganset, the world renowned "Pier,"
Was the scene. Through the lace curtained window the clear
Yellow rays of the hot August sun touched his bed
And proclaimed it was mid-day. He rose, and his head
Seemed as large and as light as an air filled balloon
While his limbs were like lead.

      In the glare of the noon,
The follies of night show their makeup, and seem
Like hideous monsters evoked by some dream.

The sea called to Roger: "Come, lie on my breast
And forget the dull world. My unrest shall give rest
To your turbulent feelings; the dregs of the wine
On your lips shall be lost in the salt touch of mine.
Come away, come away. Ah! the jubilant mirth
Of the sea is not known by the stupid old earth."

The beach swarmed with bathers--to be more exact,
Swarmed with people in costumes of bathers. In fact,
Many beautiful women bathed but in the light
Of men's eyes; and their costumes were made for the sight,
Not the sea. From the sea's lusty outreaching arms
They escaped with shrill shrieks, while the men viewed their charms
And made mental notes of them. Yet, at this hour,
The waves, too, were swelling sea meadows, a-flower
With faces of swimmers. All dressed for his bath,
Roger paused in confusion, because in his path
Surged a crowd of the curious; all eyes were bent
On the form of a woman who leisurely went
From her bathing house down to the beach. "There she goes,"
Roger heard a dame cry, as she stepped on his toes
With her whole ample weight. "What, the one with red hair?
Why, she isn't as pretty as Maude, I declare."
A man passing by with his comrade, cried: "Ned,
Look! there is La Travers, the one with the red
Braid of hair to her knees. She's a mystery here,
And at present the topic of talk at the Pier."
Roger followed their glances in time to behold
For a second a head crowned with braids of bright gold,
And a form like a Venus, all costumed in white.
Then she plunged through a billow and vanished from sight.

It was half an hour afterward, possibly more,
As Roger swam farther and farther from shore,
With new life in his limbs and new force in his brain,
That he heard, just behind him, a sharp cry of pain.
Ten strokes in the rear on the crest of a wave
Shone a woman's white face. "Keep your courage; be brave;
I am coming," he shouted. "Turn over and float."
His strong shoulder plunged like the prow of a boat

Through the billows. Six overhand strokes brought him close
To the woman, who lay like a wilted white rose
On the waves. "Now, be careful," he cried; "lay your hand
Well up on my shoulder; my arms, understand,
Must be free; do not touch them---please follow my wishes,
Unless you are anxious to fatten the fishes."
The woman obeyed him. "You need not fear me,"
She replied, "I am wholly at home in the sea.
I knew all the arts of the swimmer, I thought,
But confess I was frightened when suddenly caught
With a cramp in my knee at this distance from shore."
With slow even breast strokes the strong swimmer bore
His fair burden landward. She lay on the billows
As lightly as if she were resting on pillows
Of down. She relinquished herself to the sea
And the man, and was saved; though God knows both can be
False and fickle enough; yet resistance or strife,
On occasions like this, means the forfeit of life.
The throng of the bathers had scattered before
Roger carried his burden safe into the shore
And saw her emerge from the water, a place
Where most women lose every vestige of grace
Or of charm. But this mermaid seemed fairer than when
She had challenged the glances of women and men
As she went to her bath. Now her clinging silk suit
Revealed every line, from the throat to the foot,
Of her beautiful form. Her arms, in their splendor,
Gleamed white like wet marble. The round waist was slender,
And yet not too small. From the twin perfect crests
And the virginlike grace of her beautiful breasts
To the exquisite limbs and the curve of her thigh,
And the arch of her proud little instep, the eye
Drank in beauty. Her face was not beautiful; yet

The gaze lingered on it, for Eros had set
His seal on her features. The mouth full and weak,
The blue shadow drooping from eyelid to cheek
Like a stain of crushed grapes, and the pale, ardent skin,
All spoke of volcanic emotions within.

By her tip tilted nose and low brow, it was plain
To read how her impulses ruled o'er her brain.
She had given the chief role of life to her heart,
And her intellect played but a small minor part.
Her eyes were the color the sunlight reveals
When it pierces the soft, furry coat of young seals.
The thickly fringed lids seemed unwilling to rise,
But drooped, half concealing them; wonderful eyes,
Full of secrets and bodings of sorrow. As coarse
And as thick as the mane of a finely groomed horse
Was her bright mass of hair. The sea, with rough hands,
Had made free with the braids, and unloosened the strands
Till they hung in great clusters of curls to her knees.
Her voice, when she spoke, held the breadth and the breeze
Of the West in its tones; and the use of the ***R***
Made the listener certain her home had been far
From New England. Long after she vanished from view
The eye and the ear seemed to sense her anew.
There was that in her voice and her presence which hung
In the air like a strain of a song which is sung
By a singer, and then sings itself the whole day,
And will hot be silenced.

   As birds flock away
From meadow to tree branch, now there and now here,
So, from beach to Casino, each day at the Pier
Flock the gay pleasure seekers. The balconies glow

With beauty and color. The belle and the beau
Promenade in the sunlight, or sit tete-a-tete,
While the chaperons gossip together. Bands play,
Glasses clink; and 'neath sheltering lace parasols
There are plans made for meeting at drives or at balls.

Roger gat at a table alone, with his glass
Of mint julep before him, and watched the crowd pass.
There were all sorts of people from all sorts of places.
He thought he liked best the fair Baltimore faces.
The South was the land of fair women, he mused,
Because they were indolent. Women who used
Mind or body too freely. Changed curves into angles,
For beauty forever with intellect wrangles.
The trend of the fair sex to-day must alarm
Every lover of feminine beauty and charm.

As he mused Roger watched with a keen interest
For a sight of his Undine. "All coiffured and drest,
With her wonderful body concealed, and her hair
Knotted up, well, I doubt if she seem even fair,"
He soliloquized. "Ah!" the word burst from his lips,
For he saw her approaching. She walked from the hips
With an undulous motion. As graceful and free
From all effort as waves swinging in from the sea
Were her movements. Her full molded figure seemed slight
In its close fitting gown of black cloth; and the white
Of her cheek seemed still whiter by contrast. Her clothes
Were tasteful and quiet; yet Roger Montrose
Knew in some subtle manner he could not express
('Tis an instinct men have in the matters of dress)
That they never were made in New York. By her hat
One can oft read a woman's whole character. That

Which our fair Undine wore was a thing of rich lace,
Flowers and ribbons like others one saw in the place.
Yet the width of the brim, or the twist of its bows,
Or the way it was worn made it different from those.
As it drooped o'er the eyes full of mystery there,
It seemed, all at once, both a menace and dare;
A menace to women, a dare to the men.
She bowed as she passed Roger's table; and then
Took a chair opposite, spread her shade of red silk,
Called a waiter and ordered a cup of hot milk,
Which she leisurely sipped. She seemed unaware
Of the curious eyes she attracted. Her air
Was of one quite at home, and entirely at ease
With herself, the sole person she studied to please.
She had been for three weeks at the Pier, and alone,
Without maid or escort, and nothing was known
Of her there, save the name which the register bore,
"Mrs. Travers, New York." Men were mad to learn more
But the women were distant. One can't, at such places,
Accept as credentials good figures or faces.
There was an unnameable *something* about
Mrs. Travers which filled other women with doubt
And all men with interest. Roger, blase,
Disillusioned with life as he was, felt the sway
Of her strong personality, there as she sat
Looking out 'neath the rim of her coquettish hat
With dark eyes on the sea. Few people had power
To draw his gray thoughts from himself for an hour
As this woman had done; she was food for his mind,
And he sought by his inner perceptions to find
in what class she belonged. "An adventuress? No,
Though I fancy three-fourths of the women think so
And one-half of the men; but that role leaves a trace,

An expression, I fail to detect in her face.
Her past is not shadowed; my judgment would say
That her sins lie before her, and not far away.
She's a puzzle, I think, to herself; and grim Fate
Will aid her in solving the riddle too late.
Her soul dreams of happiness; but in her eyes
The sensuous foe to all happiness lies.
As the rain is drawn up by some moods of the sun,
Some natures draw trouble from life; her's is one."

She rose and passed by him again, and her gown
Brushed his knee. A light tremor went shivering down
His whole body. She left on the air as she went
A subtle suggestion of perfume; the scent
Which steals out of some fans, or old laces, and seems
Full of soft fragrant fancies and languorous dreams.
She haunted the mind, though she passed from the sight.
When Roger Montrose sought his pillow that night,
'Twas to dream of La Travers. He thought she became
A burning red rose, with each leaf like a flame.
He stooped down and plucked it, and woke with a start,
As it turned to an adder and struck at his heart.

The dream left its impress, as certain dreams should,
For, as warnings of evil, precursors of good,
They are sent to our souls o'er a mystical line,
Night messages, couched in a cipher divine.

Roger knew much of life, much of women, and knew
Even more of himself and his weaknesses. Few
Of us mortals look inward; our gaze is turned out
To watch what the rest of the world is about,
While the rest of the world watches us.

     Roger's reason
And logic were clear. But his will played him treason.
If you looked at his hand, you would see it. Hands speak
More than faces. His thumb (the first phalanx) was weak,
Undeveloped; the second, firm jointed and long,
Which showed that the reasoning powers were strong,
But the will, from disuse, had grown feeble.

     That morning
He looked on his dream in the light of a warning
And made sudden plans for departure. "To go
Is to fly from some folly," he said, "for I know
What salt air and dry wine, and the soft siren eyes
Of a woman, can do under midsummer skies
With a man who is wretched as I am. Unrest
Is a tramp, who goes picking the locks on one's breast
That a whole gang of vices may enter. A thirst
For strong drink and chance games, those twin comrades accursed,
Are already admitted. Oh Mabel, my wife,
Reach, reach out your arms, draw me into the life
That alone is worth living. I need you to-day,
Have pity, and love me, oh love me, I pray.
I will turn once again from the bad world to you.
Though false to myself, to my vows I am true."

When a soul strives to pull itself up out of sin
The devil tries harder to push it back in.
And the man who attempts to retrace the wrong track
Needs his God and his will to stand close at his back.

Through what are called accidents, Roger was late
At the train. Are not accidents servants of Fate?
The first coach was filled; he passed on to the second.

That, too, seemed complete, but a gentleman beckoned
And said, "There's a seat, sir; the third from the last
On your left." Roger thanked him and leisurely passed
Down the aisle, with his coat on his arm, to the place
Indicated. The seat held a lady, whose face
Was turned to the window. "Pray pardon me, miss"
(For he judged by her back she was youthful), "is this
Seat engaged?" As he spoke, the face turned in surprise,
And Roger looked into the long, languid eyes
Of La Travers. She smiled, moved her wraps from the seat,
And he sat down beside her. The same subtle, sweet
Breath of perfume exhaled from her presence, and made
The place seem a boudoir. The deep winey shade
'Neath her eyes had grown larger, as if she had wept
Or a late, lonely vigil with memory kept.

A man who has rescued a woman from danger
Or death, does not seem to her wholly a stranger
When next she encounters him; yet both essayed
To be formal and proper; and each of them made
The effort a failure. The jar of a train
At times holds a mesmeric spell for the brain
And a tense excitation for nerves; and the shriek
Of the engine compels one to lean near to speak
Or to list to his neighbor. Formality flies
With the smoke of the train and floats off to the skies.
Roger led his companion to talk; and the theme
Which he chose, was herself, her life story. The dream
Of the previous night was forgotten. The charm
Of the woman outweighed superstitious alarm.

When the sunlight began to play peek-a-boo
Through the tunnels, which told them the journey was through,

Roger looked at his time-piece; the train for Bay Bend
Left in just twenty minutes; but what a rude end
To the day's pleasant comradeship--rushing away
With a hurried good-bye! He decided to stay
Over night in the city. He was not expected
At home. Mrs. Travers was quite unprotected,
And almost a stranger in Gotham. He ought
To see her safe into her doorway, he thought.
At the doorway she gave him her hand, with a smile;
"I have known you," she said, "such a brief little while,
Yet you seem like a friend of long standing; I say
Good-bye with reluctance."

   "Perhaps, then, I may
Call and see you to-morrow?" the words seemed to fall
Of themselves from his lips; words he longed to recall
When once uttered, for deep in his conscience he knew
That the one word for him to speak now, was adieu.
The lady's soft, cushion-like hand rested still
In his own, and the contact was pleasant. A thrill
From the finger tips quickened his pulses.

   "You may
Call to-morrow at four." The soft hand slipped away
And left his palm lonely.

   "The call must be brief,"
He said to himself, with a sense of relief,
As he ran down the steps, "for at five my train goes."
Yet the five o'clock train bore no Roger Montrose
From New York. Mrs. Travers had asked him to dine.
A tete-a-tete dinner with beauty and wine,
To stir the man's senses and deaden his brain.

(The devil keeps always good chefs in his train.)
It was ten when he rose for departure. The room
Seemed a garden of midsummer fragrance and bloom.
The lights with their soft rosy coverings made
A glow like late sunsets, in some tropic glade.
The world seemed afar, with its dullness and duty,
And life was a rapture of love and of beauty.

God knows how it happened; they never knew how.
He turned with a formal conventional bow,
And some well chosen words of politeness, to go.
Her mouth was a rose Love had dropped in the snow
Of her face. It smiled up to him, luscious and sweet.
In the tip of each finger he felt his heart beat,
Like five hearts all in one, as her hand touched his own.
She murmured "good-night," in a tremulous tone.
White, intense, through the soft golden mist which the wine
Had cast over his vision, he saw her face shine.
Her low lidded eyes held a lion-like glow.
You have seen sudden storms lash the ocean? You know
How the cyclone, unheralded, rises in wrath,
And leaves devastation and death in its path?
So swift, sudden passion may rise in its power,
And ruin and blight a whole life in an hour.
Two unanchored souls in its maelstrom were whirled,
Drawn down by love's undertow, lost to the world.
The dark, solemn billows of night shut them in.
Like corpses afloat on the ocean of sin
They must seem to their true, better selves, when again
The tide drifts them back to the notice of men.

Forget me, dear; forget and cease to love me,
I am not worth one memory, kind or true,
Let silent, pale Oblivion spread above me
Her winding sheet, for I am dead to you.
Forget, forget.

Sin has resumed its interrupted story;
I am enslaved, who dreamed of being free.
Say for my soul, in life's dark purgatory,
One little prayer, then cease to think of me.
Forget, forget.

I ask you not to pity or to pardon;
I ask you to forget me. Tear my name
From out your heart; the wound will heal and harden.
Death does not dig so deep a grave as shame.
Forget, forget.

VIII.

Roger's Letter to Mabel.

Farewell! I shall never again seek your side;
I will stay with my sins and leave you with your pride.
Let the swift flame of scorn dry the tears of regret,
Shut me out of your life, lock the door and forget.
I shall pass from your skies as a vagabond star
Passes out of the great solar system afar
Into blackness and gloom; while the heavens smile on,
Scarce knowing the poor erring creature is gone.
Say a prayer for the soul sunk in sinning; I die
To you, and to all who have known me. Good-bye.

Mabel's Letter to Maurice.

I break through the silence of years, my old friend,
To beg for a favor; oh, grant it! I send
Roger's letter in confidence to you, and ask,
In the name of our sweet early friendship, a task,
Which, however painful, I pray you perform.
Poor Roger! his bark is adrift in the storm.
He has veered from the course; with no compass of faith
To point to the harbor, he goes to his death.
You are giving your talents and time, I am told,
To aiding the poor; let this victim of gold
Be included. His life has not learned self-control,
And luxury stunted the growth of his soul.
In blindness of spirit he took the wrong track,

But he sees his great error and longs to come back.
Oh, help me to reach him and save him, Maurice.
My heart yearns to show him the infinite peace
Found but in God's love. Let us pity, forgive
And help him, dear friend, to seek Christ and to live
In the light of His mercy. I know you will do
What I ask, you were ever so loyal and true.

Maurice to Mabel.

Though bitter the task (why, your heart must well know),
Your wish shall be ever my pleasure. I go
On the search for the prodigal. Not for his sake,
But because you have asked me, I willingly make
This effort to find him. Sometimes, I contend,
It is kinder to let a soul speed to the end
Of its swift downward course than to check it to-day,
But to see it to-morrow pursue the same way.
The man who could wantonly stray from your side
Into folly and sin has abandoned all pride.
There is little to hope from him. Yet, since his name
Is the name you now bear, I will save him from shame,
God permitting. To serve and obey you is still
Held an honor, Madame, by Maurice Somerville.

Maurice to Mabel Ten Days Later.

The search for your husband is finished. Oh, pray
Tear all love and all hope from your heart ere I say
What I must say. The man has insulted your trust;
He has dragged the most sacred of ties in the dust,
And ruined the fame of a woman who wore,
Until now, a good name. He has gone. Close the door

Of your heart in his face if he seeks to come back.
The sleuth hounds of justice were put on his track,
And his life since he left you lies bare to my gaze.
He sailed yesterday on the "Paris." For days
Preceding the journey he lived as the guest
Of one Mrs. Zoe Travers, who comes from the West!
A widow, young, fair, well-connected. I hear
He followed her back to New York from the Pier,
And now he has taken the woman abroad.
My letter sounds brutal and harsh. Would to God
I might soften the facts in some measure; but no,
In matters like this the one thing is to know
The whole truth, and at once. Though the pain be intense
It pulls less on the soul than the pangs of suspense.
Like a surgeon of fate, with my pen for a knife,
I cut out false hopes which endanger your life.
Let the law, like a nurse, cleanse the wound--there is shame
And disgrace for you now in the man's very name.
Though justice is blindfolded, yet she can hear
When the chink of gold dollars sounds close in her ear.

One needs but to give her this musical hint
To save you the sight of your sorrows in print.
Closed doors, private hearing; a sentence or two
In the journals; then dignified freedom for you.
When love, truth and loyalty vanish, the tie
Which binds man to woman is only a lie.
Undo it! remember at all times I stand
As a friend to rely on--a serf to command.

* * * * *

Some women there are who would willingly barter
A queen's diadem for the crown of a martyr.
They want to be pitied, not envied. To know
That the world feels compassion makes joy of their woe;
And the keenest delight in their misery lies,
If only their friends will look on with wet eyes.

In fact, 'tis the prevalent weakness, I find,
Of the sex. As a mass, women seem disinclined
To be thought of as happy; they like you to feel
That their bright smiling faces are masks which conceal
A dead hope in their hearts. The strange fancy clings
To the mind of the world that the rarest of things--
Contentment--is commonplace; and, that to shine
As something superior, one must repine,
Or seem to be hiding an ache in the breast.
Yet the commonest thing in the world is unrest,
If you want to be really unique, go along
And act as if Fate had not done you a wrong,
And declare you have had your deserts in this life.

The part of the patient, neglected young wife
Contained its attractions for Mabel Montrose.
She was one of the women who live but to pose
In the eyes of their friends; and she so loved her art
That she really believed she was living the part.
The suffering martyr who makes no complaint
Was a role more important, by far, than the saint
Or reformer. As first leading lady in grief,
Her pride in herself found a certain relief.

The ardent and love-selfish husband had not
Been so dear to her heart, or so close to her thought,
As this weak, reckless sinner, who woke in her soul
Its dominant wish--to reform and control.

(How often, alas, the reformers of earth,
If they studied their purpose, would find it had birth
In this thirst to control; in the poor human passion
The minds and the manners of others to fashion!

We sigh o'er the heathen, we weep o'er his woes,
While forcing him into our creeds and our clothes.
If he adds our diseases and vices as well,
Still, at least we have guided him into *our* hell
And away from his own heathen hades. The pleasure
Derived from that thought but reformers can measure.)

The thing Mabel Montrose loved best on this earth
Was a sinner, and Roger but doubled his worth
In her eyes when he wrote her that letter. And still
When the last message came from Maurice Somerville
And the bald, ugly facts, unsuspected, unguessed,
Lay before her, the *woman* awoke in her breast,
And the patient reformer gave way to the wife,
Who was torn with resentment and jealousy's strife.
Ah, jealousy! vain is the effort to prove
Your right in the world as the offspring of love;
For oftener far, you are spawned by a heart
Where Cupid has never implanted a dart.
Love knows you, indeed, for you serve in his train,
But crowned like a monarch you royally reign
Over souls wherein love is a stranger.

       No thought
Came to Mabel Montrose that her own life was not
Free from blame. (How few women, indeed, think of this
When they grieve o'er the ruin of marital bliss!)
She was shocked and indignant. Pain gave her a new
Role to play without study; she missed in her cue
And played badly at first, was resentful and cried
Against Fate for the blow it had dealt to her pride
(Though she called it her love), and declared her life blighted.
It is one thing, of course, for a wife to be slighted
For the average folly the world calls a sin,
Such as races, clubs, games; when a woman steps in
The matter assumes a new color, and Mabel,
Who dearly loved sinners, at first seemed unable
To pardon, or ask God to pardon, the crime
Of her husband; an angry disgust for a time
Drove all charity out of her heart. For a thief,
For a forger, a murderer, even, her grief
Had been mingled with pity and pardon; the one
Thing she could not forgive was the thing he had done.
It was wicked, indecent, and so unrefined.
To the lure of the senses her nature was blind,
And her mantle of charity never had been
Wide enough to quite cover that one vulgar sin.

In the letter she sent to Maurice, though she said
Little more than her thanks for his kindness, he read
All her tense nervous feelings between its few lines.
Though we study our words, the keen reader divines
What we *thought* while we penned them; thought odors reveal
What words not infrequently seek to conceal.

Maurice read the grief, the resentment, the shame

Which Mabel's heart held; to his own bosom came
Stealing back, masked demurely as friendly regard,
The hope of a lover--that hope long debarred.
His letters grew frequent; their tone, dignified,
Unselfish, and manly, appealed to her pride.
Sweet sympathy mingled with praise in each line
(As a gentle narcotic is stirred into wine),
Soothed pain, stimulated self love, and restored her
The pleasure of knowing the man still adored her.

Understand, Mabel Montrose was not a coquette,
She lacked all the arts of the temptress; and yet
She was young, she was feminine; love to her mind
Was extreme admiration; it pleased her to find
She was still, to Maurice, an ideal. A woman
Must be quite unselfish, almost superhuman,
And full of strong sympathy, who, in her soul,
Feels no wrench when she knows she has lost all control
O'er the heart of a man who once loved her.

      Months passed,
And Mabel accepted her burden at last
And went back to her world and its duties. Her eyes,
Seemed to say when she looked at you, "please sympathize,
On the slight graceful form or the beautiful face.
Twas a sorrow of mind, not a sorrow of heart,
And the two play a wholly dissimilar part
In the life of a woman.

      Maurice Somerville
Kept his place as good friend through sheer force of his will
But his heart was in tumult; he longed for the time
When, free once again from the legalized crime

Of her ties, she might listen to all he would say.
There was anguish, and doubt, and suspense in delay,
Yet Mabel spoke never of freedom. At length
He wrote her, "My will has exhausted its strength.
Read the song I enclose; though my lips must be mute,
The muse may at least improvise to her lute."

Song.

There was a bird as blithe as free,
  (Summer and sun and song)
She sang by the shores of a laughing sea,
And oh, but the world seemed fair to me,
  And the days were sweet and long.

There was a hunter, a hunter bold,
  (Autumn and storm and sea)
And he prisoned the bird in a cage of gold,
And oh, but the world grew dark and cold,
  And the days were sad to me.

The hunter has gone; ah, what cares he?
  (Winter and wind and rain)
And the caged bird pines for the air and the sea,
And I long for the right to set her free
  To sing in the sun again.

The hunter has gone with a sneer at fate,
  (Spring and the sea and the sun)
Let the bird fly free to find her mate,
Ere the year of love grow sere and late.
  Sweet ladye, my song is done.

Mabel's Letter to Maurice.

To the song of your muse I have listened. Oh, cease
To think of me but as a friend, dear Maurice.
Once a wife, a wife alway. I vowed from my heart,
"For better, for worse, until death do us part."
No mention was made in the service that day
Of breaking my fetters if joy flew away.
"For better, for worse," a vow lightly spoken,
When Fate brings the "worse," how lightly 'tis broken!

The "worse," in my case, is the worst fate can give.
Tho' I shrank from the blow, I must bear it and live,
Not for self, but for duty; nor strive to evade
Fulfilling the promise I willingly made.
While Roger has sinned, and his sinning would be,
In the eyes of the law, proof to render me free,
It was God heard my vows and the Church sealed the bond.
Until one of us passes to death's dim beyond,
Though seas and though sins may divide us for life,
We are bound to each other as husband and wife.
In God's Court of Justice divorce is a word
Which falls without import or meaning when heard;
And the women who cast off old fetters that way,
To give place to the new, on the great Judgment Day
Must find, in the last summing up, that they stand
Side by side, in God's eyes, with the Magdalene band.
Dear Maurice, be my brother, my counselor, friend.
We are lonely without you and Ruth, at Bay Bend.
Come sometimes and brighten our lives; put away
The thoughts which are making you restless to-day
And give me your strong noble friendship; indeed
'Tis a friend that I crave, not a lover I need.

Maurice to Mabel.

You write like a woman, and one, it is plain,
Whose sentiment hangs like a cloud o'er her brain.
You gaze through a sort of traditional mist,
And behold a mirage of God's laws which exist
But in fancy. God made but one law--it is love.
A law for the earth, and the kingdoms above,
A law for the woman, a law for the man,
The base and the spire of His intricate plan
Of existence. All evils the world ever saw
Had birth in man's breaking away from this law.
God cancels a marriage when love flies away.
"Till death do us part" should be altered to say,
"Till disgust or indifference part us." I know
You never loved Roger, my heart tells me so.

He won you, I claim, through a mesmeric spell;
You dreamed of an Eden, and wakened in hell.
You pitied his weakness, you struggled to save him,
He paid with a crime the devotion you gave him.
And the blackest of insults relentlessly hurled
At your poor patient heart in the gaze of the world.
In God's mighty ledger the stroke of a pen
Has been drawn through your record of marriage. Though men
Call you wedded I hold you are widowed. Why cling
To the poor, empty, meaningless form of a thing--
To the letter, devoid of all spirit? God never
Intended a woman to hopelessly sever
Herself from all possible joy, or to make
True faithfulness suffer for faithlessness' sake.
When I think of your wrongs, when I think of my woes,
That black word divorce like a bright planet glows

In the skies of the future. Oh, Mabel, be fair
To yourself and to me. For the years of despair
I have suffered you owe me some recompense, surely.
The heart that has worshipped so long and so purely
Ought not to be slighted for mere sentiment.
We must live as our century bids us. Its bent
Is away from the worn ruts of thought. Where of old
The life of a woman was run in the mold
Of man's wishes and passions, to-day she is free;
Free to think and to act; free to do and to be
What she pleases. The poor, pining victim of fate
And man's cruelty, long ago went out of date.
In the mansion of Life there were some things askew,
Which the strong hand of Progress has righted. The new,
Better plan puts old notions of sex on the shelf.
Who is true to a knave, is untrue to herself.
Oh, be true to yourself, and have pity on one
Who has long dwelt in shadow and pines for the sun.
Love, starving on memories, begs for one taste
Of sweet hope, ere the remnant of youth goes to waste.

Mabel to Maurice.

You write like a man who sees self as his goal.
You speak of your woes--yet my travail of soul
Seems mere sentiment to you. Maurice, pause and think
Of the black, bitter potion life gave me to drink
When I dreamed of love's nectar. Too fresh is the taste
Of its gall on my lip for my heart in such haste
To reach out for the cup that is proffered anew.
A certain respect to my sorrows is due.
I am weary of love as men know it. The calm
Of a sweet, tranquil friendship would act like a balm

On the wounds of my heart; that platonic regard,
Which we read of in books, or hear sung by the bard,
But so seldom can find when we want it. I thought,
For a time, you had conquered mere self, and had brought
Such a friendship to comfort and rest me. But no,
That dream, like full many another, must go.
The love that is based on attraction of sex
Is a love that has brought me but sorrow. Why vex
My poor soul with the same thing again? If you love
With a higher emotion, you know how to prove
And sustain the assertion by conduct. Maurice,
Love must rise above passion, to infinite peace
And serenity, ere it is love, to my mind.
For the women of earth, in the ranks of mankind
There are too many lovers and not enough friends.
'Tis the friend who protects, 'tis the lover who rends.
He who *can* be a friend while he *would* be a lover
Is the rarest and greatest of souls to discover.
Have I found, dear Maurice, such a treasure in you?
If not, I must say with this letter--adieu.

As he finished the letter there seemed but one phrase
To the heart of the reader. It shone on his gaze
Bright with promise and hope. "Too fresh is the taste
Of its gall on my lip for my heart in such haste
To reach out for the cup that is offered anew."
"In such haste." Ah, how hope into certainty grew
As he read and re-read that one sentence. "Let fate
Take the whole thing in charge, I can wait--I can wait.
I have lived through the night; though the dawn may be gray
And belated, it heralds the coming of day."
So he talked with himself, and grew happy at last.
The five hopeless years of his sorrow were cast

Like a nightmare behind him. He walked once again
With a joy in his personal life, among men.
There seemed to be always a smile on his lip,
For he felt like a man on the deck of a ship
Who has sailed through strange seas with a mutinous crew,
And now in the distance sights land just in view.

The house at Bay Bend was re-opened. Once more,
Where the waves of the Sound wash the New England shore,
Walked Maurice; and beside him, young hope, with the tip
Of his fair rosy fingers pressed hard on his lip,
Urging silence. If Mabel Montrose saw the boy
With the pursed prudent mouth and the eyes full of joy
She said nothing. Grave, dignified (Ah, but so fair!),
There was naught in her modest and womanly air
To feed or encourage such hope. Yet love grew
Like an air plant, with only the night and the dew
To sustain it; while Mabel rejoiced in the friend,
Who, in spite of himself, had come back to Bay Bend,
Yielding all to her wishes. Such people, alone,
Who gracefully gave up their plans for her own,
Were congenial to Mabel. Though looking the sweet,
Fragile creature, with feminine virtues replete,
Her nature was stubborn. Beneath that fair brow
Lurked an obstinate purpose to make others bow
To herself in small matters. She fully believed
She was right, always right; and her friends were deceived,
As a rule, into thinking the same; for her eyes
Held a look of such innocent grief and surprise
When her will was opposed, that one felt her misused,
And retired from the field of dispute, self-accused.

The days, like glad children, went hurrying out
From the schoolhouse of time; months pursued the same route
More sedately; a year, then two years, passed away,
Yet hope, unimpaired, in the lover's heart lay,
As a gem in the bed of a river might lie,
Unharmed and unmoved while its waters ran by.
His toil for the poor still continued, but not
With that fervor of zeal which a dominant thought
Lends to labor. Fair love gilded dreams filled his mind,
While the corners were left for his suffering kind.
He was sorry for sorrow; but love made him glad,
And nothing in life now seemed hopeless or sad.
His tete-a-tete visits with Mabel were rare;
She ordered her life with such prudence and care
Lest her white name be soiled by the gossips. And yet,
Though his heart, like a steed checked too closely, would fret
Sometimes at these creed-imposed fetters, he felt
Keen delight in her nearness; in knowing she dwelt
Within view of his high turret window. Each day
Which gave him a glimpse of her, love laid away
As a poem in life's precious folio. Night
Held her face like a picture, dream-framed for his sight.
So he fed on the crumbs from love's table, the while
Fate sat looking on with a cynical smile.

IX.

SONGS FROM THE TURRET.

I.

In the day my thoughts are tender
  When I muse on my ladye fair.
There is never one to offend her,
  For each is pure as a prayer.
They float like spirits above her,
  About her and always near;
And they scarce dare sigh that they love her,
  Because she would blush to hear.

But in dreams my thoughts grow bolder;
  And close to my lips of fire,
I reach out my arms and enfold her,
  My ladye, my heart's desire.
And she who, in earthly places,
  Seems cold as the stars above,
Unmasks in those fair dream spaces
  And gives me love for love.

Oh day, with your thoughts of duty
  Cross over the sunset streams,
And give me the night of beauty
  And love in the Land of Dreams.
For there in the mystic, shady,
  Fair isle of the Slumber Sea,

I read the heart of my ladye
  That here she hides from me.

II.

Some day, some beauteous day,
  Joy will come back again.
Sorrow must fly away.

Hope, on her harp will play
  The old inspiring strain
Some day, some beauteous day.

Through the long hours I say,
  "The night must fade and wane,
Sorrow must fly away."

The morn's bewildering ray
  Shall pierce the night of rain,
Some day, some beauteous day.

Autumn shall bloom like May,
  Delight shall spring from pain;
Sorrow must fly away.

Though on my life, grief's gray
  Bleak shadow long hath lain,
Some day, some beauteous day,
  Sorrow must fly away.

III.

When love is lost, the day sets toward the night.
Albeit the morning sun may still be bright,
And not one cloud ship sails across the sky.
Yet from the places where it used to lie,
Gone is the lustrous glory of the light.

No splendor rests on any mountain height,
No scene spreads fair, and beauteous, to the sight.
All, all seems dull and dreary to the eye,
       When love is lost.

Love lends to life its grandeur and its might,
Love goes, and leaves behind it gloom and blight.
Like ghosts of time the pallid hours drag by,
And grief's one happy thought is that we die.
Ah! what can recompense us for its flight,
       When love is lost.

IV.

Life is a ponderous lesson book, and Fate
  The teacher. When I came to love's fair leaf
My teacher turned the page and bade me wait.
  "Learn first," she said, "love's grief";
And o'er and o'er through many a long to-morrow
  She kept me conning that sad page of sorrow.

Cruel the task; and yet it was not vain.

Now the great book of life I know by heart.
In that one lesson of love's loss and pain
　Fate doth the whole impart.
For, by the depths of woe, the mind can measure
　The beauteous unsealed summits of love's pleasure.

Now, with the book of life upon her knee,
　Fate sits! the unread page of love's delight
By her firm hand is half concealed from me,
　And half revealed to sight.
Ah Fate! be kind! so well I learned love's sorrow,
　Give me its full delight to learn to-morrow.

V.

If I were a rain drop, and you were a leaf,
　I would burst from the cloud above you
And lie on your breast in a rapture of rest,
　And love you, love you, love you.

If I were a brown bee, and you were a rose,
　I would fly to you, love, nor miss you;
I would sip and sip from your nectared lip,
　And kiss you, kiss you, kiss you.

If I were a doe, dear, and you were a brook,
　Ah, what would I do then, think you?
I would kneel by your bank, in the grasses dank,
　And drink you, drink you, drink you.

VI.

Time owes me such a heavy debt,
  How can he ever make things right?
For suns that with no promise set
  To help me greet the morning light,

For dreams that no fruition met,
  For joys that passed from bud to blight,
Time owes me such a heavy debt;
  How can he ever make things right?

For passions balked, with strain and fret
  Of hopes delayed, or perished quite,
For kisses that I did not get
  On many a love impelling night,
Time owes me such a heavy debt;
  How can he ever make things right?

VII.

As the king bird feeds on the heart of the bee,
So would I feed on the sweets of thee.

As the south wind kisses the leaf at will,
From the leaf of thy lips I would drink my fill.

As the sun pries into the heart of a rose,
I would pry in thy heart, and its thoughts disclose.

As a dewdrop mirrors the loving sky,
I would see myself in thy tear wet eye.

As the deep night shelters the day in its arms,
I would hide thee, dear, from the world's alarms.

VIII.

Now do I know how Paradise doth seem,
Now do I know the deep red depths of hell.
Swift from those fair supernal heights I fell
To burning flames of hades, in a dream.
Methought my ladye rested by a stream
Which rippled through the verdure of a dell.
She lay like Eve; dear God, I dare not tell
Of her perfections; of the glow and gleam
Of tinted flesh, and undulating hair,
Of sudden thigh, and sweetly rounded breast.
Then, like a cloud, he came, from God knows where,
And on her eyes and mouth mad kisses pressed.
I fell, and fell, through leagues of scorching space,
And always saw his lips upon her face.

IX.

Love is the source of all supreme delight,
  Love is the bitter fountain of despair;
Who follows Love shall stand upon the height,
  Yet through the darkest depths, Love, too, leads there.

Courage needs he who would with bold Love fare,
  Let him set forth with all his strength bedight;
Yet in his heart this song to banish care--
  "Love is the source of all supreme delight."

And he must sing this song both day and night,
  Though he be led down shadowy pathways where
Black waters moan, through valleys struck with blight,
  "Love is the bitter fountain of despair."

Let him be brave, and bravely let him dare
  Whate'er betide, and feel no coward fright.
Who shares the worst, the best deserves to share;
  Who follows Love shall stand upon the height.

Ah! sweet is peace to those who faced the fight,
  And bright the crown those faithful ones shall wear,
Who whispered, when the shadows veiled their sight,
  "Yet through the darkest depths, Love, too, leads there."

To hearts that best know Love, his dark is fair,
  His sorrow gladness, and his wrong is right.
All joys lie waiting on his winding stair;
  All ways, ail paths of Love lead to the light.
            Love is the source.

X.

My ladye's eyes are wishing wells,
  Wherein I gaze with silent yearning;
Deep in their depths my future dwells.

My ladye's eyes are wishing wells,
But not one sign my fate foretells,
  While my poor heart with love is burning.
My ladye's eyes are wishing wells,
  Wherein I gaze with silent yearning.

XI.

Three things my ladye seemeth like to me--
She seems like moonlight on a waveless sea.

And like the delicate fragrance, which exhales,
When Day's warm garments brush the dewy vales.

And when my heart grows weary of earth's sound,
She seems like silence--restful and profound.

XII.

The moon flower, grown from a slip so slender,
  Has burst in a star bloom, full and white.
The air is filled with a perfume tender,
  The breath that blows from that garden height.
  Yet moments lag that should take their flight
On wings, like the wings of a homing dove,
  And the world goes wrong where it should go right,
For this is a night that is lost to love.

Again, like a queen, who would rashly spend her

Dower of wealth in a single night,
The proud moon seems, on her track of splendor,
 Enriching the world with her silver light.
 She flings on the crest of each billow a bright
Pure gem, from the casket of jewels above.
 But I sigh as I gaze on the glorious sight,
"This is a night that is lost to love."

Oh, I would that the moon might never wend her
 Way through the skies in royal might,
Till the haughty heart of my lady surrender
 And the faithful love of a life requite.
 For the moon was made for a lover's delight;
And grayer than gloom must its luster prove
 To the soul that sighs under sorrow's blight,
"This is a night that is lost to love."

L'Envoi.

Fate, have pity upon my plight,
 And the heart of my lady to mercy move.
For the saddest words that youth can write
 Are, "This is a night that is lost to love."

XIII.

As the waves of the outgoing sea
 Leave the rocks and the drift wood bare,
When your thoughts are for others than me,
 My heart is the strand of despair--

Beloved,
  Where bleak suns glare,
And Joy, like a desolate mourner, gropes
In the wrecks of broken hopes.

As the incoming waves of the sea,
  The rocks and the sandbar hide,
When your thoughts flow back to me,
  My heart leaps up on the tide--
        Beloved,
  Where my glad hopes ride
With joy at the wheel, and the sun above
In a glorious sky of love.

XIV.

There was a bard all in the olden time,
  When bards were men to whom the world gave ear,
And song an art the great gods deemed sublime,
  Who sought to make his willful lady hear
By weaving strange new melodies of rhyme,
  Which voiced his love, his sorrow, and his fear.

Sweetheart, my soul is heavy now with fear,
  Lest thou shalt frown upon me for all time.
Ah! would that I had skill to weave a rhyme
  Worthy to win the favor of thine ear.
Tho' all the world were deaf, if thou didst hear
  And smile, my song would seem to me sublime.

But ah! too vast, too awful and sublime,
  Is my great passion, born of grief and fear,
To clothe in verse. Why, if the world could hear
  And understand my love, then for all time,
So long as there was sound or listening ear,
  All space would ring and echo with my rhyme.

Such passion seems belittled by a rhyme--
It needs the voice of nature. The sublime,
  Loud thunder crash, that hurts the startled ear,
  And stirs the heart with awe, akin to fear,
The weird, wild winds of equinoctial time;
  These voices tell my love, wouldst thou but hear.

And listening at the flood tides, thou might'st hear
  The love I bear thee surging through the rhyme
  Of breaking billows, many a moon full time.
  Why, I have heard thee call the sea sublime,
When every wave but voiced the anguished fear
Of my man's heart to thy unconscious ear.

Vain, then, the hope that thou wilt lend thine ear
To any song of mine, or deign to hear
My lays of longing or my strains of fear.
  Vain is the hope to weave for thee a rhyme,
  Or sweet or sad, or subtle or sublime,
  Which wins thy gracious favor for all time.

Oh, cruel time! my lady will not hear,
  Though in her ear love sings a song sublime,
And my sad rhyme ends, like my love, in fear.

Bright like the comforting blaze on the hearth,
Sweet like the blooms on the young apple tree,
Fragrant with promise of fruit yet to be
Are the home-keeping maidens of earth.

Better and greater than talent is worth,
And where is the glory of brush or of pen
Like the glory of mothers and molders of men--
The home-keeping women of earth?

Crowned since the great solar system had birth,
They reign unsurpassed in their beautiful sphere.
They are queens who can look in God's face without fear--
The home-keeping women of earth.

X.

A man whose mere name was submerged in the sea
Of letters which followed it, B. A., M. D.,
And Minerva knows what else, held forth at Bellevue
On what he believed some discovery new
In medical Science (though, mayhap, a truth
That was old in Confucius' earliest youth),
And a bevy of bright women students sat near,
Absorbing his wisdom with eye and with ear.

Close by, lay the corpse of a man, half in view.
Dear shades of our dead and gone grandmamas! you
Whose modesty hung out red flags on each cheek,
Danger signals--if some luckless boor chanced to speak
The words "leg" or "liver" before you, I think
Your gray ashes, even, would deepen to pink
Should your ghost happen into a clinic or college
Where your granddaughters congregate seeking for knowledge.
Forced to listen to what they are eager to hear,
No doubt you would fancy the world out of gear,
And deem modesty dead, with last century belles.

Honored ghosts, you, would err! for true modesty dwells
In the same breast with knowledge, and takes no offense.
Truth never harmed anything yet but pretense.

There are fashions in modesty; what in your time
Had been deemed little less than an absolute crime
In matters of dress, or behavior, to-day
Is the custom. And however daring you may
Deem our manners and modes, yet, were facts fully known,
Our morals compare very well with your own.

The women composing the class at Bellevue
Were young--under thirty; some pleasing to view,
Some plain. Roman features prevailed, with brown hair,
But one was so feminine, soft eyed and fair
That she seemed out of place in a clinic, as though
A rose in a vegetable garden should grow.
While her face was intelligent, none would avow
That cold intellect dwelt on that fair oval brow,
Or looked out of the depths of those golden gray eyes,
The color of smoke against clear, sunny skies.

'Twas a warm woman face, made for fireside nooks,
Not a face to be bent over medical books.
There was nothing aggressive in features or form;
She was meant for still harbors, and not for the storm
And the strife of rude waters. The swell of her breast
Suggested love's sweet downy cushion of rest
For the cheeks of fair children. Her plump little hands,
Seemed fashioned for sewing small gussets and bands
And fussing with laces and ribbons, instead
Of cutting cold flesh and dissecting the dead.
And yet, as a student she ranked with the first.
But conscience, in labor once chosen, not thirst
For such knowledge, had spurred her to action. This day
She seemed inattentive, her air was distrait,
As if thought had slipped free of the bridle and rein
And galloped away over memory's plain.

It was true; it was strange, too, but there in the class,
While the learned man was talking, her mind seemed to pass
Out, away from the clinic, away from the town,
To a New England midsummer garden close down
By the salt water's edge; and she felt the wind blowing
Among her loose locks as she leaned o'er her sewing,
While the voice of a man stirred her heart into song.
She was called from her dream by the clang of the gong
Which foretells an arrival at Bellevue. The class
Was dismissed for the day. In the hall, forced to pass
By the stretcher (low brougham of misery), she
Whom we know was Ruth Somerville, looked down to see
The white, haggard face of the man whom her mind
Had strayed off in a waking day vision to find
But a moment before.

The wild, passionate cry
Which arose in her heart, was held back, nor passed by
The white sentinels set on her lip. The serene,
Lofty look which deep feeling controlled gives the mien
Marked her air as she turned to the surgeon and said:
"This man lying here, either dying or dead,
Was a classmate, at Yale, of my brother's; my friend
Is his wife. Let me stay by his side to the end,
If the end has not come."

          It was Roger Montrose,
Grown old with his sins and grown gaunt with his woes,
Lying low in his manhood before her.

          His eyes
Opened slowly; a wondering look of surprise
Met the soft orbs above him. "Ruth--Ruth Somerville,"
He said feebly. "Tell Mabel"--then sighed, and was still.

But it was not the stillness of death. There was life
In that turbulent heart yet; that heart torn with strife,
Scarred with passion, and wracked by the pangs of remorse.
"Death's swift leaden messenger missed in its course
By the breadth of a hair," said the surgeon. "The ball
Lies in there by the shoulder. His chances are small
For a new start on earth. While a sober man might
Hope to conquer grim Death in this hand-to-hand fight,
Here old Alcohol stands as Death's second, fierce, cruel,
And stronger than Life's one aid, skill, in the duel.
You tell me the wife of this man is your friend?
He was shot by a woman, who then made an end
Of her own life. I hope it was not----" "Oh, no--no,
Not his wife," Ruth replied, "for he left her to go

With this other, his victim--poor creature--they say
She was good till she met him. Ah! what a black way
For love's rose scented path to lead down to, and end.
God pity her, pity her." "Her, not your friend?
Not his wife?"

      There was gentle reproof in the tone
Of the staid old physician. Ruth's eyes met his own
In brave, silent warfare; the blue and the gray
Again faced each other in battle array.

Ruth:

I pity the woman who suffered. His wife
Goes her way well contented. Love was in her life
But an incident; while to this other, dear God,
It was all; on what sharp, burning ploughshares she trod,
Down what chasms she leaped, how she tossed the whole world,
Like a dead rose, behind her, to lie and be whirled
In the maelstrom of love for one moment. Ah, brief
Is the rapture such souls find, and long is their grief,
Black their sin, blurred their record, and scarlet their shame.
And yet when I think of them, sorrow, not blame,
Stirs my being. Blind passion is only the weed
Of fair, beautiful love. Both are sprung from one seed;
One grows wild, one is trained and directed. Condemn
The hand that neglected--but ah! pity *them*.

Surgeon:

You speak with much feeling. But now, if the friends
Of this man are to see him before his life ends
I recommend action on your part. His stay

On this planet, I fear, will be finished to-day.
A man who neglects and abuses his wife,
Who gives her at best but the dregs of his life,
In the hey day of health, when he's drained his last cup
Has a fashion of wanting to settle things up.
Craves forgiveness, and hopes with a few final tears
To wash out the sins and the insults of years.
Call your friend; bid her hasten, lest lips that are dumb,
Having wasted life's feast, shall refuse her death's crumb.

Ruth:

There are souls to whom crumbs are sufficient, at least
They seem not to value love's opulent feast.
They neglect, they ignore, they abuse, or destroy
What to some poor starved life had been earth's rarest joy.
'Tis a curious fact that love's banqueting table
Full often is spread for the guest the least able
To do the feast justice. The gods take delight
In offering crusts to the starved appetite
And rich fruits, to the sated or sickly.

      The eyes
Of the surgeon were fixed on Ruth's face with a wise
Knowing look in their depths, and he said to himself,
"There's a mystery here which young Cupid, sly elf,
Could account for. I judge by her voice and her face
That the wife of this man holds no very warm place
In Miss Somerville's heart, though she names her as friend.
Ah, full many a drama has come to an end
'Neath the walls of Bellevue, and the curtain will fall
On one actor to-night; though the audience call,
He will make no response, once he passes from view,

For Death is the prompter who gives him the cue."

The wisest minds err. When a clergyman tries
To tell a man where he will go when he dies,
Or when a physician makes bold to aver
Just the length of a life here, both usually err.
So it is not surprising that Roger, at dawn,
Sat propped up by pillows, still haggard and wan,
But seemingly stronger, and eager to tell
His story to Ruth ere the death shadows fell.

"If I go before Mabel can reach me," he sighed,
"Tell her this: that my heart was all hers when I died,
Was all hers while I lived. Ah! I see how you start,
But that other--God pity her--not with my heart,
But my sensual senses I loved her. The fire
Of her glance blinded men to all things save desire.
It called to the beast chained within us. Her lips
Held the nectar that makes a man mad when he sips.
Her touch was delirium. In the fierce joys
Of her kisses there lurked the fell curse which destroys
All such rapture--satiety. When passion dies,
And the mind finds no pleasure, the spirit no ties
To replace it, disgust digs its grave. Ay! disgust
Is ever the sexton who buries dead lust.

When two people wander from virtue's straight track,
One always grows weary and longs to go back.
Well, I wearied. God knows how I struggled to hide
The truth from the poor, erring soul at my side.
And God knows how I hated my life when I first
Found that passion's mad potion had palled on my thirst.
Once false to my virtues, now false to my sin,

I seemed less to myself than I ever had been.
We parted. This bullet hole here in my breast
Proceeds with the story and tells you the rest.
She smiled, I remember, in saying adieu:
Then two swift, sharp reports--and I woke in Bellevue
With one ball in my breast.

Ruth:

     And the other in hers.
No more with wild sorrow that sad bosom stirs.
She is dead, sir, the woman you led to her ruin.

Roger:

The woman led me. Ah! not all the undoing
In these matters lies at man's door. In the mind
Of full many a so-called chaste woman we find
Unchaste longings. The world heaps on man its abuse
When he woos without wedding; yet women seduce
And betray us; they lure us and lead us to shame;
As they share in the sin, let them share in the blame.

Ruth:

Hush! the woman is dead.

Roger:

     And I dying. But truth
Is not changed by the death of two people! Oh, Ruth,
Be just ere you judge me! the death of my child
Half unbalanced my reason; weak, wretched and wild

With drink and with sorrows, the devil's own chance
Flung me down by the side of a woman whose glance
Was an opiate, lulling the conscience. I fell,
With the woman who tempted me, down to dark hell.
In the honey of sin hides the sting of the bee.
The honey soon sated--the sting stayed with me.
Like a damned soul I looked from my Hades, above
To the world I had left, and I craved the pure love
That but late had seemed cold, unresponsive. Her eyes,
Mabel's eyes, shone in dreams from the far distant skies
Of the lost world of goodness and virtue. Like one
Who is burning with thirst 'neath a hot desert sun,
I longed for her kiss, cool, reluctant, but pure.
Ah! man's love for good women alone can endure,
For virtue is God, the Eternal. The rest
Is but chaos. The worst must give way to the best.
Tell Mabel--Ruth, Ruth, she is here, oh thank God.

She stood, like a violet sprung from the sod,
By his bedside; pale, beautiful, dewy with tears.
The spectre of death bridged the chasm of years:
He sighed on her bosom. "Forgive, oh forgive!"
She kissed his pale forehead and answered him: "Live,
Live, my husband! oh plead with the angels to stay
Until God, too, has pardoned your sins. Let us pray."

Ruth slipped from the room all unnoticed. She seemed
Like a sleeper who wakens and knows he has dreamed
And is dazed with reality. On, as if led
By some presence unseen, to the inn of the dead
She passed swiftly; the pale silent guest whom she sought
Lay alone on her narrow and unadorned cot.
No hand had placed blossoms about her; no tear

Of love or of sorrow had hallowed that bier.
The desperate smile life had left on her face
Death retained; but he touched, too, her brow with a grace
And a radiance, subtle, mysterious. Under
The half drooping lids lay a look of strange wonder,
As if on the sight of those sorrowing eyes
The unexplored country had dawned with surprise.

The pure, living woman leaned over the dead,
Lovely sinner, and kissed her. "God rest you," she said.
"Poor suffering soul, you were forged in that Source
Where the lightnings are fashioned. Love guided, your force
Would have been like a current of life giving joys,
And not like the death dealing bolt which destroys.
Oh, shame to the parents who dared give you birth,
To live and to love and to suffer on earth,
With the serious lessons of life unexplained,
And your passionate nature untaught and untrained.
You would not lie here in your youth and your beauty
If your mother had known what was motherhood's duty.
The age calls to woman, "Go, broaden your lives,"
While for lack of good mothers the Potter's Field thrives.
But you, poor unfortunate, you shall not lie
In that dust heap of death; while the summers roll by
You shall sleep where green hillsides are kissed by the wave,
And the soft hand of pity shall care for your grave.

XI.

Ruth's Letter to Maurice, Six Months Later.

The springtime is here in our old home again,
Which again you have left. Oh, most worthy of men,
Why grieve for unworthiness? Why waste your life
For a woman who never was meant for a wife?
Mabel Lee has no love in her nature. Your heart
Would have starved in her keeping. She plays her new part,
As the faithful, forgiving, sweet spouse, with content.
I think she is secretly glad Roger went
Astray for a season. She stands up still higher
On her pedestal, now, for Bay Bend to admire.
She is pleased with herself. As for Roger, he trots
Like a lamb in her wake, with the blemishing spots
Of his sins washed away by the Church. Oh I seem
To myself, in these days, like one waked from a dream
To blessed reality. Off in the Bay
I saw a fair snowy sailed ship yesterday.
The masts shone like gold, and the furrowed waves laughed,
To be beat into foam by the beautiful craft.
But close in the harbor I saw the ship lying;
What seemed like the wings of a sea gull when flying,
Were weather stained sheets; there were no masts of gold,
And the craft was uncleanly, unseaworthy, old.
Well, the man whom I loved, and loved vainly, and whom
I fancied had shadowed my whole life with gloom,
Has been shown to my sight like that ship in the Bay,
And all my illusions have vanished away.

The man is by nature weak, selfish, unstable.
I think if some woman more loving than Mabel,
More tender, more tactful, less painfully good,
Had directed his home-life, perchance Roger would
Have evolved his best self, that pure atom of God,
Which lies deep in each heart like a seed in the sod.
'Tis the world's over-virtuous women, ofttimes,
Who drive men of weak will into sexual crimes.
I pity him. (God knows I pity, each, all
Of the poor striving souls who grope blindly and fall
By the wayside of life.) But the love which unbidden
Crept into my heart, and was guarded and hidden
For years, that has vanished. It passed like a breath,
In the gray Autumn morning when Roger faced death,
As he thought, and uncovered his heart to my sight.
Like a corpse, resurrected and brought to the light,
Which crumbles to ashes, the love of my youth
Crumbled off into nothingness. Ah, it is truth;
Love can die! You may hold it is not the true thing,
Not the genuine passion, which dies or takes wing;
But the soil of the heart, like the soil of the earth,
May, at varying times of the seasons, give birth
To bluebells, and roses, and bright goldenrod.
Each one is a gift from the garden of God,
Though it dies when its season is over. Why cling
To the withered dead stalk of the blossoms of spring
Through a lifetime, Maurice? It is stubbornness only,
Not constancy, which makes full many lives lonely.
They want their own way, and, like cross children, fling
Back the gifts which, in place of the lost flowers of spring,
Fate offers them. Life holds in store for you yet
Better things, dear Maurice, than a dead violet,
As it holds better things than dead daisies for me.

To Roger Montrose, let us leave Mabel Lee,
With our blessing. They seem to be happy; or she
Seems content with herself and her province; while he
Has the look of one who, overfed with emotion,
Tries a diet of spiritual health-food, devotion.
He is broken in strength, and his face has the hue
Of a man to whom passion has bidden adieu.
He has time now to worship his God and his wife.
She seems better pleased with the dregs of his life
Than she was with the bead of it.

      Well, let them make
What they will of their future. Maurice, for my sake
And your own, put them out of your thoughts. All too brief
And too broad is this life to be ruined by grief
Over one human atom. Like mellowing rain,
Which enriches the soil of the soul and the brain,
Should the sorrow of youth be; and not like the breath
Of the cyclone, which carries destruction and death.
Come, Maurice, let philosophy lift you above
The gloom and despair of unfortunate love.
Sometimes, if we look a woe straight in the face,
It loses its terrors and seems commonplace;
While sorrow will follow and find if we roam.
Come, help me to turn the old house into home.
We have youth, health, and competence. Why should we go
Out into God's world with long faces of woe?
Let our pleasures have speech, let our sorrows be dumb,
Let us laugh at despair and contentment will come.
Let us teach earth's repiners to look through glad eyes,
For the world needs the happy far more than the wise.
I am one of the women whose talent and taste
Lie in home-making. All else I do seems mere waste

Of time and intention; but no woman can
Make a house seem a home without aid of a man.
He is sinew and bone, she is spirit and life.
Until the veiled future shall bring you a wife,
Me a mate (and both wait for us somewhere, dear brother),
Let us bury old corpses and live for each other.
You will write, and your great heart athrob through your pen
Shall strengthen earth's weak ones with courage again.
Where your epigrams fail, I will offer a pill,
And doctor their bodies with "new woman" skill.
(Once a wife, I will drop from my name the M. D.
I hold it the truth that no woman can be
An excellent wife and an excellent mother,
And leave enough purpose and time for another
Profession outside. And our sex was not made
To jostle with men in the great marts of trade.
The wage-earning women, who talk of their sphere,
Have thrown the domestic machine out of gear.
They point to their fast swelling ranks overjoyed;
Forgetting the army of men unemployed.

The banner of Feminine "Rights," when unfurled,
Means a flag of distress to the rest of the world.
And poor Cupid, depressed by such follies and crimes,
Sits weeping, alone, in the Land of Hard Times.
The world needs wise mothers, the world needs good wives,
The world needs good homes, and yet woman strives
To be everything else but domestic. God's plan
Was for woman to rule the whole world, ***through a man***.
There is nothing a woman of sweetness and tact
Can not do without personal effort or act.
She needs but infuse lover, husband or son
With her own subtle spirit, and lo! it is done.

Though the man is unconscious, full oft, of the cause,
And fancies himself the sole maker of laws.
Well, let him. The cannon, no doubt, is the prouder
For not knowing its noise is produced by the powder.
Yet this is the law: ***Who can love, can command***.)
But I wander too far from the subject in hand,
Which is, your home coming. Make haste, dear; I find
More need every day of your counseling mind.
I work well in harness, but poorly alone.
Until that bright day when Fate brings us our own,
Let us labor together. I see many ways,
Many tasks, for the use of our talents and days.
Your wisdom shall better the workingmen's lives,
While I will look after their daughters and wives,
And teach them to cook without waste; for, indeed,
It is knowledge like this which the poor people need,
Not the stuff taught in schools. You shall help them to think,
While I show them what they can eat and can drink
With least cost, and most pleasure and benefit. Please
Write me and say you will come, dear Maurice.
Home, sister, and duty are all waiting here;
Who keeps close to duty finds pleasure dwells near.

XII.

Maurice's Letter to Ruth:

No, no. I have gambled with destiny twice,
And have staked my whole hopes on a home; but the dice
Thrown by Fate made me loser. Henceforward, I know
My lot must be homeless. The gods will it so.

I fought, I rebelled; I was bitter. I strove
To outwit the great Cosmic Forces, above,
Or beyond, or about us, who guide and control
The course of all things from the moat to the soul.

The river may envy the peace of the pond,
But law drives it out to the ocean beyond.
If it roars down abysses, or laughs through the land,
It follows the way which the Forces have planned.

So man is directed. His only the choice
To help or to hinder--to weep or rejoice.
But vain is refusal--and vain discontent,
For at last he must walk in the way that was meant.

My way leads through shadow, alone to the end
I must work out my karma, and follow its trend.
I must fulfill the purpose, whatever it be,
And look not for peace till I merge in God's sea.

Though bankrupt in joy, still my life has its gain;

I have climbed the last round in the ladder of pain.
There is nothing to dread. I have drained sorrow's cup
And can laugh as I fling it at Fate bottom up.

I have missed what I sought; yet I missed not the whole.
The best part of love is in loving. My soul
Is enriched by its prodigal gifts. Still, to give
And to ask no return, is my lot while I live.

Such love may be blindness, but where are love's eyes?
Such love may be folly, love seldom is wise.
Such love may be madness, was love ever sane?
Such love must be sorrow, for all love is pain.

Love goes where it must go, and in its own season.
Love cannot be banished by will or by reason.
Love gave back your freedom, it keeps me its slave.
I shall walk in its fetters, unloved, to my grave.

So be it. What right has the ant, in the dust,
To cry that the world is all wrong, and unjust,
Because the swift foot of a messenger trod
Down the home, and the hopes, that were built in the sod?

What is man but an ant, in this universe scheme?
Though dear his ambition, and precious his dream,
God's messengers speed all unseen on their way,
And the plans of a lifetime go down in a day.

No matter. The aim of the Infinite mind,
Which lies back of it all, must be great, must be kind.
Can the ant or the man, though ingenious and wise,
Swing the tides of the sea--set a star in the skies?

Can man fling a million of worlds into space,
To whirl on their orbits with system and grace?
Can he color a sunset, or create a seed,
Or fashion one leaf of the commonest weed?

Can man summon daylight, or bid the night fall?
Then how dare he question the Force which does all?
Where so much is flawless, where so much is grand,
All, all must be right, could our souls understand.

Ah, man, the poor egotist! Think with what pride
He boasts his small knowledge of star and of tide.
But when fortune fails him, or when a hope dies,
The Maker of stars and of seas he denies!

I questioned, I doubted. But that is all past;
I have learned the true secret of living at last.
It is, to accept what Fate sends, and to know
That the one thing God wishes of man--is to grow.

Growth, growth out of self, back to him--the First Cause:
Therein lies the purpose, the law of all laws.
Tears, grief, disappointment, well, what are all these
To the Builder of stars and the Maker of seas?

Does the star long to shine, when He tells it to set,
As the heart would remember when told to forget?
Does the sea moan for flood tide, when bid to be low,
As a soul cries for pleasure when given life's woe?

In the Antarctic regions a volcano glows,
While low at its base lie the up-reaching snows.

With patient persistence they steadily climb,
And the flame will be quenched in the passage of time.

My heart is the crater, my will is the snow,
Which yet may extinguish its volcanic glow.
When self is once conquered, the end comes to pain,
And that is the goal which I seek to attain.

I seek it in work, heaven planned, heaven sent;
In the kingdom of toil waits the crown of content.
Work, work! ah, how high and divine was its birth,
When God, the first laborer, fashioned the earth.

The world cries for workers; not toilers for pelf,
But souls who have sought to eliminate self.
Can the lame lead the race? Can the blind guide the blind?
We must better ourselves ere we better our kind.

There are wrongs to be righted; and first of them all,
Is to lift up the leaners from Charity's thrall.
Sweet, wisdomless Charity, sowing the seed
Which it seeks to uproot, of dependence and need.

For vain is the effort to give man content
By clothing his body, by paying his rent.
The garment re-tatters, the rent day recurs;
Who seeks to serve God by such charity errs.

Give light to the spirit, give strength to the mind,
And the body soon cares for itself, you will find.
First, faith in God's wisdom, then purpose and will,
And, like mist before sunlight, shall vanish each ill.

To the far realm of Wisdom there lies a short way.
To find it we need but the password--Obey.
Obey like the acorn that falls to the sod,
To rise, through the heart of the oak tree, to God.

Though slow be the rising, and distant the goal,
Serenity waits at the end for each soul.
I seek it. Not backward, but onward I go,
And since sorrow means growth, I will welcome my woe.

In the ladder of lives we are given to climb,
Each life counts for only a second of time.
The one thing to do in the brief little space,
Is to make the world glad that we ran in the race.

No soul should be sad whom the Maker deemed worth
The great gift of song as its dower at birth.
While I pass on my way, an invisible throng
Breathes low in my ear the new note of a song.

So I am not alone; for by night and by day
These mystical messengers people my way.
They bid me to hearken, they bid me be dumb
And to wait for the true inspiration to come.

The Codes Of Hammurabi And Moses
W. W. Davies

QTY

The discovery of the Hammurabi Code is one of the greatest achievements of archaeology, and is of paramount interest, not only to the student of the Bible, but also to all those interested in ancient history...

Religion   **ISBN:** *1-59462-338-4*   **Pages:132**

MSRP $12.95

The Theory of Moral Sentiments
Adam Smith

QTY

This work from 1749. contains original theories of conscience amd moral judgment and it is the foundation for systemof morals.

Philosophy   **ISBN:** *1-59462-777-0*   **Pages:536**

MSRP $19.95

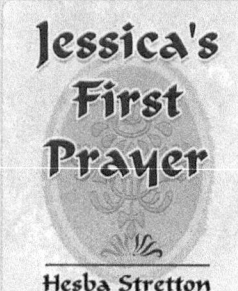

Jessica's First Prayer
Hesba Stretton

QTY

In a screened and secluded corner of one of the many railway-bridges which span the streets of London there could be seen a few years ago, from five o'clock every morning until half past eight, a tidily set-out coffee-stall, consisting of a trestle and board, upon which stood two large tin cans, with a small fire of charcoal burning under each so as to keep the coffee boiling during the early hours of the morning when the work-people were thronging into the city on their way to their daily toil...

Childrens   **ISBN:** *1-59462-373-2*

Pages:84

MSRP $9.95

My Life and Work
Henry Ford

QTY

Henry Ford revolutionized the world with his implementation of mass production for the Model T automobile. Gain valuable business insight into his life and work with his own auto-biography... "We have only started on our development of our country we have not as yet, with all our talk of wonderful progress, done more than scratch the surface. The progress has been wonderful enough but..."

Pages:300

Biographies/   **ISBN:** *1-59462-198-5*   *MSRP $21.95*

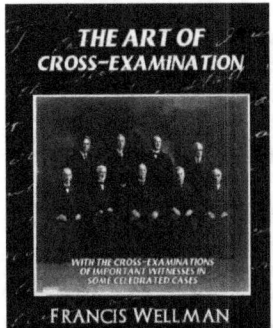

The Art of Cross-Examination
Francis Wellman

QTY

I presume it is the experience of every author, after his first book is published upon an important subject, to be almost overwhelmed with a wealth of ideas and illustrations which could readily have been included in his book, and which to his own mind, at least, seem to make a second edition inevitable. Such certainly was the case with me; and when the first edition had reached its sixth impression in five months, I rejoiced to learn that it seemed to my publishers that the book had met with a sufficiently favorable reception to justify a second and considerably enlarged edition. ..

Pages:412

Reference   ISBN: *1-59462-647-2*   *MSRP $19.95*

On the Duty of Civil Disobedience
Henry David Thoreau

QTY

Thoreau wrote his famous essay, On the Duty of Civil Disobedience, as a protest against an unjust but popular war and the immoral but popular institution of slave-owning. He did more than write—he declined to pay his taxes, and was hauled off to gaol in consequence. Who can say how much this refusal of his hastened the end of the war and of slavery ?

Law   ISBN: *1-59462-747-9*   **Pages:48**

MSRP $7.45

Dream Psychology Psychoanalysis for Beginners
Sigmund Freud

QTY

Sigmund Freud, born Sigismund Schlomo Freud (May 6, 1856 - September 23, 1939), was a Jewish-Austrian neurologist and psychiatrist who co-founded the psychoanalytic school of psychology. Freud is best known for his theories of the unconscious mind, especially involving the mechanism of repression; his redefinition of sexual desire as mobile and directed towards a wide variety of objects; and his therapeutic techniques, especially his understanding of transference in the therapeutic relationship and the presumed value of dreams as sources of insight into unconscious desires.

Pages:196

Psychology   ISBN: *1-59462-905-6*   *MSRP $15.45*

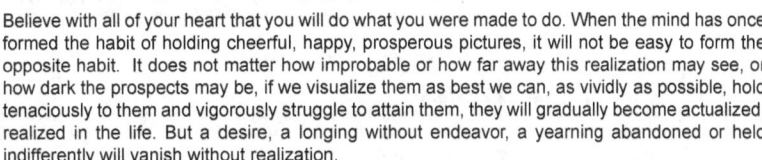

The Miracle of Right Thought
Orison Swett Marden

QTY

Believe with all of your heart that you will do what you were made to do. When the mind has once formed the habit of holding cheerful, happy, prosperous pictures, it will not be easy to form the opposite habit. It does not matter how improbable or how far away this realization may see, or how dark the prospects may be, if we visualize them as best we can, as vividly as possible, hold tenaciously to them and vigorously struggle to attain them, they will gradually become actualized, realized in the life. But a desire, a longing without endeavor, a yearning abandoned or held indifferently will vanish without realization.

Pages:360

Self Help   ISBN: *1-59462-644-8*   *MSRP $25.45*

QTY

The Rosicrucian Cosmo-Conception Mystic Christianity *by Max Heindel* ISBN: *1-59462-188-8* **$38.95**
The Rosicrucian Cosmo-conception is not dogmatic, neither does it appeal to any other authority than the reason of the student. It is: not controversial, but is: sent forth in the, hope that it may help to clear... New Age/Religion Pages 646

Abandonment To Divine Providence *by Jean-Pierre de Caussade* ISBN: *1-59462-228-0* **$25.95**
"The Rev. Jean Pierre de Caussade was one of the most remarkable spiritual writers of the Society of Jesus in France in the 18th Century. His death took place at Toulouse in 1751. His works have gone through many editions and have been republished... Inspirational/Religion Pages 400

Mental Chemistry *by Charles Haanel* ISBN: *1-59462-192-6* **$23.95**
Mental Chemistry allows the change of material conditions by combining and appropriately utilizing the power of the mind. Much like applied chemistry creates something new and unique out of careful combinations of chemicals the mastery of mental chemistry... New Age Pages 354

The Letters of Robert Browning and Elizabeth Barret Barrett 1845-1846 vol II ISBN: *1-59462-193-4* **$35.95**
by Robert Browning and Elizabeth Barrett Biographies Pages 596

Gleanings In Genesis (volume I) *by Arthur W. Pink* ISBN: *1-59462-130-6* **$27.45**
Appropriately has Genesis been termed "the seed plot of the Bible" for in it we have, in germ form, almost all of the great doctrines which are afterwards fully developed in the books of Scripture which follow... Religion/Inspirational Pages 420

The Master Key *by L. W. de Laurence* ISBN: *1-59462-001-6* **$30.95**
In no branch of human knowledge has there been a more lively increase of the spirit of research during the past few years than in the study of Psychology, Concentration and Mental Discipline. The requests for authentic lessons in Thought Control, Mental Discipline and... New Age/Business Pages 422

The Lesser Key Of Solomon Goetia *by L. W. de Laurence* ISBN: *1-59462-092-X* **$9.95**
This translation of the first book of the "Lemegton" which is now for the first time made accessible to students of Talismanic Magic was done, after careful collation and edition, from numerous Ancient Manuscripts in Hebrew, Latin, and French... New Age/Occult Pages 92

Rubaiyat Of Omar Khayyam *by Edward Fitzgerald* ISBN:*1-59462-332-5* **$13.95**
Edward Fitzgerald, whom the world has already learned, in spite of his own efforts to remain within the shadow of anonymity, to look upon as one of the rarest poets of the century, was born at Bredfield, in Suffolk, on the 31st of March, 1809. He was the third son of John Purcell... Music Pages 172

Ancient Law *by Henry Maine* ISBN: *1-59462-128-4* **$29.95**
The chief object of the following pages is to indicate some of the earliest ideas of mankind, as they are reflected in Ancient Law, and to point out the relation of those ideas to modern thought. Religion/History Pages 452

Far-Away Stories *by William J. Locke* ISBN: *1-59462-129-2* **$19.45**
"Good wine needs no bush, but a collection of mixed vintages does. And this book is just such a collection. Some of the stories I do not want to remain buried for ever in the museum files of dead magazine-numbers an author's not unpardonable vanity..." Fiction Pages 272

Life of David Crockett *by David Crockett* ISBN: *1-59462-250-7* **$27.45**
"Colonel David Crockett was one of the most remarkable men of the times in which he lived. Born in humble life, but gifted with a strong will, an indomitable courage, and unremitting perseverance... Biographies/New Age Pages 424

Lip-Reading *by Edward Nitchie* ISBN: *1-59462-206-X* **$25.95**
Edward B. Nitchie, founder of the New York School for the Hard of Hearing, now the Nitchie School of Lip-Reading, Inc, wrote "LIP-READING Principles and Practice". The development and perfecting of this meritorious work on lip-reading was an undertaking... How-to Pages 400

A Handbook of Suggestive Therapeutics, Applied Hypnotism, Psychic Science ISBN: *1-59462-214-0* **$24.95**
by Henry Munro Health/New Age/Health/Self-help Pages 376

A Doll's House: and Two Other Plays *by Henrik Ibsen* ISBN: *1-59462-112-8* **$19.95**
Henrik Ibsen created this classic when in revolutionary 1848 Rome. Introducing some striking concepts in playwriting for the realist genre, this play has been studied the world over. Fiction/Classics/Plays 308

The Light of Asia *by sir Edwin Arnold* ISBN: *1-59462-204-3* **$13.95**
In this poetic masterpiece, Edwin Arnold describes the life and teachings of Buddha. The man who was to become known as Buddha to the world was born as Prince Gautama of India but he rejected the worldly riches and abandoned the reigns of power when... Religion/History/Biographies Pages 170

The Complete Works of Guy de Maupassant *by Guy de Maupassant* ISBN: *1-59462-157-8* **$16.95**
"For days and days, nights and nights, I had dreamed of that first kiss which was to consecrate our engagement, and I knew not on what spot I should put my lips..." Fiction/Classics Pages 240

The Art of Cross-Examination *by Francis L. Wellman* ISBN: *1-59462-309-0* **$26.95**
Written by a renowned trial lawyer, Wellman imparts his experience and uses case studies to explain how to use psychology to extract desired information through questioning. How-to/Science/Reference Pages 408

Answered or Unanswered? *by Louisa Vaughan* ISBN: *1-59462-248-5* **$10.95**
Miracles of Faith in China Religion Pages 112

The Edinburgh Lectures on Mental Science (1909) *by Thomas* ISBN: *1-59462-008-3* **$11.95**
This book contains the substance of a course of lectures recently given by the writer in the Queen Street Hall, Edinburgh. Its purpose is to indicate the Natural Principles governing the relation between Mental Action and Material Conditions... New Age/Psychology Pages 148

Ayesha *by H. Rider Haggard* ISBN: *1-59462-301-5* **$24.95**
Verily and indeed it is the unexpected that happens! Probably if there was one person upon the earth from whom the Editor of this, and of a certain previous history, did not expect to hear again... Classics Pages 380

Ayala's Angel *by Anthony Trollope* ISBN: *1-59462-352-X* **$29.95**
The two girls were both pretty, but Lucy who was twenty-one who supposed to be simple and comparatively unattractive, whereas Ayala was credited, as her Bombwhat romantic name might show, with poetic charm and a taste for romance. Ayala when her father died was nineteen... Fiction Pages 484

The American Commonwealth *by James Bryce* ISBN: *1-59462-286-8* **$34.45**
An interpretation of American democratic political theory. It examines political mechanics and society from the perspective of Scotsman James Bryce Politics Pages 572

Stories of the Pilgrims *by Margaret P. Pumphrey* ISBN: *1-59462-116-0* **$17.95**
This book explores pilgrims religious oppression in England as well as their escape to Holland and eventual crossing to America on the Mayflower, and their early days in New England... History Pages 268

QTY

The Fasting Cure *by Sinclair Upton* ISBN: *1-59462-222-1* **$13.95**
In the Cosmopolitan Magazine for May, 1910, and in the Contemporary Review (London) for April, 1910, I published an article dealing with my experiences in fasting. I have written a great many magazine articles, but never one which attracted so much attention... New Age/Self Help/Health Pages 164

Hebrew Astrology *by Sepharial* ISBN: *1-59462-308-2* **$13.45**
In these days of advanced thinking it is a matter of common observation that we have left many of the old landmarks behind and that we are now pressing forward to greater heights and to a wider horizon than that which represented the mind-content of our progenitors... Astrology Pages 144

Thought Vibration or The Law of Attraction in the Thought World ISBN: *1-59462-127-6* **$12.95**
by William Walker Atkinson Psychology/Religion Pages 144

Optimism *by Helen Keller* ISBN: *1-59462-108-X* **$15.95**
Helen Keller was blind, deaf, and mute since 19 months old, yet famously learned how to overcome these handicaps, communicate with the world, and spread her lectures promoting optimism. An inspiring read for everyone... Biographies/Inspirational Pages 84

Sara Crewe *by Frances Burnett* ISBN: *1-59462-360-0* **$9.45**
In the first place, Miss Minchin lived in London. Her home was a large, dull, tall one, in a large, dull square, where all the houses were alike, and all the sparrows were alike, and where all the door-knockers made the same heavy sound... Childrens/Classic Pages 88

The Autobiography of Benjamin Franklin *by Benjamin Franklin* ISBN: *1-59462-135-7* **$24.95**
The Autobiography of Benjamin Franklin has probably been more extensively read than any other American historical work, and no other book of its kind has had such ups and downs of fortune. Franklin lived for many years in England, where he was agent... Biographies/History Pages 332

Name	
Email	
Telephone	
Address	
City, State ZIP	

☐ **Credit Card**   ☐ **Check / Money Order**

Credit Card Number	
Expiration Date	
Signature	

Please Mail to: Book Jungle
PO Box 2226
Champaign, IL 61825
or Fax to: 630-214-0564

ORDERING INFORMATION

web: *www.bookjungle.com*
email: *sales@bookjungle.com*
fax: *630-214-0564*
mail: *Book Jungle PO Box 2226 Champaign, IL 61825*
or PayPal *to sales@bookjungle.com*

Please contact us for bulk discounts